BILGE
WATER
BONES

To Dea,
Run wild!

BILGE
WATER
BONES

by
Glynn Marsh Alam

[signature: Glynn M Alam]

MEMENTO MORI MYSTERIES
New York

Memento Mori Mysteries
Published by
Avocet Press Inc
19 Paul Court, Pearl River, NY 10965
http://www.avocetpress.com
mysteries@avocetpress.com

AVOCET PRESS

This novel is a work of fiction and each character in it is fictional. No reference to any living person is intended or should be inferred.

Library of Congress Cataloging-in-Publication Data
Alam, Glynn Marsh, 1943-
  Bilge water bones : a Luanne Fogarty mystery / Glynn Marsh Alam.-- 1st ed.
     p. cm.
  ISBN 0-9725078-4-1
 1. Fogarty, Luanne (Fictitious character)--Fiction. 2. Women detectives--Florida--Tallahassee Region--Fiction. 3. Tallahassee Region (Fla.)--Fiction. 4. Missing persons--Fiction. 5. Women divers--Fiction. I. Title.
  PS3551.L213B555 2004
  813'.54--dc22

     2004007274

Printed in the USA
First Edition

To the memory of Ralph Dyment, detective, mentor, friend.

The waters of the South are like its people, with dangerous undercurrents and a deep beauty. And like the people, they hide ghosts that ride the surface in the early morning mists when the water is warmer than the air. Sometimes the mists sweep through the palmetto bushes on shore and creep between the heavy oaks like a grand lady's white handkerchief, folding in and out, rising from the forest floor now, crawling back into the bottom scrub, only to reappear on the front porch and lie in wait for the blistering sun to evaporate all but the memory. Sometimes the memory lingers longer, restless in the minds of the people inside the house. We all live with ghosts. Some of us die with them.

CHAPTER ONE

Some people say Jimmy Hoffa is buried down here in a sinkhole, weighted down with chains and cement. Seems one of the suspicious characters surrounding his disappearance moved to the area a few years back. Locals started with the rumors that he'd been tossed to the gators who frequent Tallahassee watering holes.

I'm not sure about Hoffa, but I do know a good many others have found their eternal niche where cold waters swirl over blue flesh. The fish eventually turn them into white bones that blend in with the limestone cave walls. Unless, of course, they're stuck on the side of a sinkhole, entangled in tree limbs that jut out from the dark earth like a spider web. The bones don't get so bright and white there, not for many years.

In spite of the wet blanket heat that rested on the Palmetto River surface, underwater cold pressed against my skin, penetrating the diving suit that was meant to protect for only a few hours. I had dived three times, keeping up the pace with two other sheriff's department divers, searching a few deep caves as well as shallow trenches where eel and hydrilla grass competed to entangle my scuba gear.

A half mile down the river, the curious lined the bridge over the brackish water that led to the Gulf of Mexico. Most were fishermen or tourists whose jaunts on the river had to be postponed while the sheriff's divers did their duty. We were just as much entertainment as their efforts at catching local bass might have been, but

11

we couldn't equal the excitement of a bridge looky-loo suddenly
spying a floater. You could tell by their bodies bent over the railing,
even some sneaking down the bank until they reached the yellow
police tape. Somebody hoped to be the hero of the day.

"You okay, Luanne?" Deputy Loman, a large man with sleepy
eyes and no sense of balance, lowered a lukewarm orange soda to
me at the edge of the dock. He stumbled backward when he stood
up straight.

"Are you?" He grabbed at air and finally steadied himself. I figured it was the eyes and looking at water for a length of time. It
disrupted his inner ear or something like that.

"Amado's on his way from Tallahassee. Said if you don't find
the body by four, we're putting off the search until tomorrow."

I nodded, sat the drink on the edge of the dock and slid the
mask back over my face. I'd give it one more try. Losing a teenage
life in a swimming hole is not unusual, but losing his body is another problem, especially when he's from a class A family of real
estate developers in town and stirring up all kinds of scandal at his
parents' river retreat. Tommy Hanover had been reported as having been quite inebriated after grad night. He piled himself and two
girls in a sports boat, and turned sharp angles in waters where manatee often get slashed on sharp propellers. He finally hit one, tossing
all three teenagers into the river currents. The girls managed to find
the shore, but Tommy was gone. The boat, its motor bent and the
front end smashed, hugged the oak it had hit when it sped ashore
without a pilot. The massive body of a fat manatee, its bulby head
shredded, floated a few feet from the dock until Fish and Game
tossed a net and dragged it ashore.

"Where are the kid's parents?" I asked.

"The mother is back at her cabin with some neighbors. Father is
over there, pacing." Loman nodded toward the mass of marked

cars and equipment wagons that lined the high bank behind police tape. Our diving trailer sat there, too. We had been called in before dawn.

"Hit a manatee at that speed, it's going to rock the boat all right," said Tony Amado, sheriff's detective and the best Cuban good ol' boy south of Atlanta. Early that morning, he had paced the sandy shore, barely getting his black wing tips damp. He jabbed a finger at the spots where he thought we should dive. "Some old rotting boats over there." He had pointed to a cove heavy with foliage. "And some more a ways down. Might have been caught up in the debris."

By noon, the wrecked boat had been surrounded with scene tape. Vernon Drake, my diving partner underwater, and lover above, rested on the cement dock, a private structure built by another monied family a few houses down from the teen's. The third diver, a wounded man in body and diving, sat aside from us, rubbing his face with a towel.

"Is he really up to this?" I had asked Tony when we were first called in on the dive. "He hasn't done much since the injury." I was talking about Harry MacAllister, a former lover, archeology professor, and all round great diver. He had been badly wounded in an underwater cave bombing and had lost his nerve. He still wouldn't go into caves.

"You guys do the holes," said Tony. "MacAllister is trying to ease back into the job. He's okay in the open areas."

I shrugged. Maybe Tony was a good guy after all. He always deferred to Harry in the past, using me—a woman after all—as a backup adjunct diver.

After Tony left the scene, Harry moved silently under the water, sifting through the heavy grass and shining a light into cave entrances. If the space was deep enough for a body to be pushed by the current, he waved the light for me and Vernon to head inside.

At two, we met at the edge of the dock. Harry shoved his mask on top of his head and leaned his face into the sun. The thick salt-and-pepper hair had become mostly salt now, and the crow's-feet at the edges of his eyes had grown into the hairline. He let out a sigh.

"Is your leg hurting?" I asked.

Harry opened his eyes and blinked at me. "Whole body is hurt-ing. I'm cold." He reached toward the ladder and climbed out, stum-bling slightly as he put weight on the injured leg.

I climbed after him and sat on the edge of the dock. Vernon, his mask shoved to the top of his bald head, tread water and grinned at me.

"You too tired to go on?" he asked.

"Let's follow the currents," I said. "It seems to me they head into that cove over there." I pointed to the heavy oak growth that hung over the river like a huge cape, its moss touching the surface. "It leads into Grandpa's Creek. There's debris from old boats that the kid could have been caught on."

Vernon hooked his finger in a "follow me" attitude. I pushed my mask over my eyes and rolled into the water, leaving Harry to lay flat on the dock, his wet suit unzipped to expose his skin to the hot sun.

We swam through shallow water and heavy grass until we reached the shadows of the trees. The water deepened and the grass cleared but there was no body. We followed the lane where the banks nar-rowed then opened again into the creek. The water was murky but shallow enough in spots to notice a human male body if one was there. We passed a canoe that had sunk some seasons back, its sides rotting and the bottom loaded with river mud.

A red buoy floated above us, signaling the depths to any boaters who might pull into this area. I felt currents pushing against my fins and let them guide my movements. A stream of cold water shot suddenly from deep holes in the bottom, limestone caves that meandered beneath the land until they reached the Gulf. Vernon worked a few feet away on the other side of the lane. Maybe a body could be pushed here, but I doubted it. The currents coming from the river weren't strong enough.

The water darkened at one spot, signaling a drop of several feet. That's where I spied the boat. It had sunk, its stern hidden in the mud and debris and darkness. The bow pointed upwards, but it wouldn't be noticed at the surface unless someone stood directly over the spot. It was at least a thirty footer, one that would have been used for weekend sports fishing. The bow and the bottom near it was damaged. Gashes that appeared clean as though they had been made by some steel edge made large gapes where small fish darted in and out like underwater performers.

I swam to the top and touched a rough edge. The material fell off and drifted away in the currents, changing the opening from fist to basketball size. I shined my light into the bilge where leaves and mud had taken up residence. The engine blended in with the mud, but behind it, something stood out, its color a stark white against the dark brown of the boat parts. I stuck my arm into the bilge up to the elbow and waved the water in front of the color. A grin took form as the mud moved aside. It was a row of teeth inside a rounded skull. I got the eerie feeling of being grinned at by a blind man for the eye sockets bulged with mud.

I motioned to Vernon who took a look and gave the surface signal. Back at the dock, Loman met us again.

"That it for the day?" He stood next to Harry who still basked in the sun.

"We found a body," I said. "But it's not Tommy Hanover's."

CHAPTER TWO

"You got your poor people back on Grandpa's Creek," said Pasquin, his octogenarian voice telling the story of the river he'd lived with all his life. He was my Cajun neighbor and best friend who often sat on my front porch after a ride on currents. He knew all, even about the people who had more recently invaded this swamp south of Tallahassee. "They don't have the money those people down on the river have."

"And who lives back there?" I handed him an iced tea glass and joined him. We sat in rockers and watched the twilight appear in the forest, making the foliage turn black and the sky take on a red hue. My body felt unusually light and comfortable after a day in the water.

"Got me over here to pick my brain, didn't you, girl?" Pasquin sipped his tea. "Too bad about the boy." That was his only comment on Tommy Hanover. Old river men like him resented the antics of a drunken kid who played with boats and rivers like they were toys. If the forces took them out, so be it.

"We're still looking for him," I said. "If he's still alive, he's going to face one big fine for killing a manatee." But Pasquin refused to enter that conversation and returned to my question about the area.

"Couple of families got cabins there. Don't think their kids are around anymore. And some old coot who used to fix boats. Don't know if he does that anymore."

"Just three groups of people?"

"Oh, no. You got the campers who kind of live there permanently. I guess you'd call them homeless today. But they like living free and easy." He leaned back and sipped his tea. The slow rhythm of his rocking expressed his own contentment. He lived in a house not too far away, where he had it free and easy, too. He understood free and easy.

"How many?"

"How many what?"

"How many homeless or free swamp people camp back there?"

He shrugged. "Don't know. It keeps changing. They move on, you see, find a better spot, one with more fish and less people."

Pasquin wasn't going to spill the details. He talked as though I could pick up the things I wanted to know, and this made me edgy. I couldn't get impatient, just had to coax him a little more. Before I could think of the next question, he slapped his knee with the straw hat that rested there.

"And Barley Ben lives somewhere back in that neck of the woods. Done forgot about him for a while." He chuckled his secret knowledge.

"Okay, old man, tell me."

Pasquin resumed his rocking. "Got any corn bread to go with this tea?"

"Some Cajun you are. Why not beignets?" I rose to head into the kitchen.

"That'd be all right, too."

As soon as I stepped off the screened porch into the living room, the cold air conditioning hit me. It was like moving into another era, another century even. I had remodeled the place a few years back, turning it from a sagging, rotting swamp haunt to a modern dwelling that fended off the frogs and mosquitoes that inhabited my primeval forest. But these critters would never be completely vanquished. The front porch served as the link, the place where I could sit and commune with those ancient life forms that serenaded me nightly and, with their silence, warned of an approaching human.

"Will some warmed over biscuits do?" I said as I headed back to the porch. "All out of corn bread and beignets."

"Do well with a little syrup," said Pasquin as he took a biscuit from the plate.

"I knew that." I handed him a plastic bottle.

He turned the bottle over and squirted a blob of syrup onto the bread and took a bite. When he saw that I wasn't eating, he shoved the plate toward me.

"No, I ate too much after the dive."

"You want me to talk some more, right?"

I smiled. There was no fooling this man, just had to pamper him a little. "You know me too well."

"Where was I?" He dripped syrup on another biscuit.

"Barley Ben."

"Old Barley. Man never had sense enough to open the umbrella once he took it out in the rain. Tried growing turnips and some other vegetables out there in swamp mud." Pasquin stopped as though remembering something specific. A low chuckle emanated from the darkening porch.

"What?" I said.

"Barley got caught once with a mess of somebody else's fish. Took off running through the swamp with 'bout ten catfish on a string. Halfway to his shack, he got his big feet tangled up in the fish line and went rolling on the ground. Seems he was near a slough where an old gator resided. Gator sees ten fish coming at him. He opens up his mouth and swallows the whole mess." Pasquin's chuckle had turned to loud whoops. He had to take deep breaths to finish the story. "Barley got so mad he stomped into that slough and went after the gator. Sat on the critter's back and tried to yank out the fish. He finally got the string, but the green hide done chomped up the fish. And you know what old Barley did? Got his gun and hit that old gator right between the eyes."

"Was this after the laws about shooting alligators?"

"Yeah. But Barley didn't kill the thing. He hit it, and somehow broke the hide. Old gator lived for several days 'til infection killed it. Game warden got on Barley's case and fined him. He didn't pay and ended up in jail a couple of days." Pasquin let his chuckle drift into the night.

"Sounds like a lot of barleycorn to me! Where'd he get a name like that?"

Pasquin sighed. "Liked to drink the old barley whiskey. Put it away pretty good for some years there 'til he got religion. It's now and again, mostly again, these days. He's taken to preaching at most any stranger coming his way now."

"Can you tell me about any other people down that way?"

Pasquin's old voice that sounded like ocean waves on gravel turned reflective. "Long time ago during the Depression, people got desperate and put up dwellings in the swamp with whatever materials they could find. Those that could used old brick or blocks. They lasted but got covered over with vines and scrubs. You walk through that swamp and you'll find some old dwellings like that. Probably got a few rattlesnakes living inside, but you'll find them."

The night had come, making it impossible to see even the outline of the old man who rocked next to me. I heard his shoulders shrug.

"I can't remember everybody down there without seeing them. Guess you'll have to take me along."

It was my turn to chuckle. "Just what Amado ordered."

"We borrowed two divers from Franklin County." Tony stood with his hands on his hips, barking orders to uniformed deputies. Vernon and I stood with him on the cement dock. "They'll search for the kid. I want you two on the other scene."

From where we stood, we glimpsed the heavy oak grove and the river lane that moved beside it into the cove. A crane had been moved into place from the swamp side. It and three uniformed deputies were enclosed with yellow tape. The men leaned over, their backs nearly at right angles, to spy the submerged boat with its grinning occupant.

"Get suited up, take a boat and go off the side when you think you see something," said Tony. "You both got face masks and I want to hear immediately if you spy anything." He tapped the headset around his neck.

"I don't see Harry here today." I began to strip down to my bathing suit.

"Got too sore yesterday," said Tony and ground his jaw. It had to be a lie. I figured Harry had got spooked again. A flash of his former self made a sudden sadness engulf me. We had both been in that explosion, but Harry got the worst of it. He still taught his archeology classes, but for someone who had once investigated ruins in the Atlantic and mapped underwater cave systems in north Florida, his career in diving seemed doomed.

"Pasquin said he'd come along in his boat." I offered the information to Tony, knowing he would pretend to be bothered by the interfering old man, but secretly glad he was around to fill in the gaps about the folks in the area. Pasquin had been the rescuer of many a deputy, saving hours of interviews and frustrating questions. He knew the river, its waters and its shores, and most who lived there.

Vernon and I pulled on the suits that would protect us in the cold water, but would swelter us in the high heat of a Florida summer. We placed the tanks and fins into the motor boat. Vernon took the throttle.

We moved slowly to the cove where other divers were preparing to go down, take photos, then attach the hoists to pull the entire crime scene up to shore. Marshall Long, the crime scene tech who would direct his staff, sat in a folding chair he brought along. His girth, enhanced by evening meals of fried oysters and banana pudding, spread over the edges and threatened to rip apart the plastic weaving. His white coat draped over one arm of the chair. He fanned himself with a clipboard.

Vernon edged the boat as close to the far side of the lane as he could without rubbing the bank. We passed the area where the boat rested on the bottom, a skeleton grinning in its bilge, and headed down the creek that narrowed and widened, all the while covered in a canopy of oak limbs. In some of the broader areas, purple hyacinth flowers dotted the surface, their green vines forming a mass of entanglement just below the water level that could hide a water moccasin as well as a teenager. We looked for boats.

"This looks like a graveyard for canoes," said Vernon. He had stalled and was attempting to back the boat away from a thick growth of hydrilla grass. "Like they came here to die."

We tied up in a small cove and went over the side. The water was shallow, but the current moved as though the tide were coming in. In a sequence of wreckage, we found three canoes, rotting and covered in mud. The only thing that identified them were the pointed ends that poked above the river floor.

I moved to the first canoe and pushed aside the mud. It was heavy and only a small amount of debris filtered through the water. After a few moments, I could see nothing there. Vernon did the same to the second canoe. The third one looked fresher. The sides had rotted less and the mud filled only the middle. Dim letters spelled out SEYMOUR.

I headed back to the other two canoes and sifted through the mud again. The first one coughed up a piece of siding with faint letters that could have been an S and E. I tucked the wood into my mesh bag and swam toward the second canoe. The mud revealed an oar, intact but fragile. I anchored it in some eel grass while I searched for the siding with letters. It came up with a handful of hydrilla. The letters EYMO stood out clear enough to identify in the dark water.

"What's with SEYMOUR?" I asked as I dragged the oar into our motor boat.

"It's like a business, a shop somewhere that rents out to tourists or Saturday rowers." Vernon shoved his mask to the top of his head and picked up a piece of the wood. "Funny why three of their canoes would end up sunk in one spot."

Vernon pushed the boat to one side of the lane. I stuck a small flag into the bank to mark where the canoes rested. Taking the camera Tony had given me, I photographed the area.

We moved the boat at a snail's pace down the lane, leaning over the sides to spy anything from a boat to a body that might be among the swaying grasses. The river floor got closer and closer until the creek was no longer navigable. Scuba gear would be useless here.

Near the end, the water became a muddy mess of foliage and finally disappeared into heavy forest growth. In the grass at the edge, I spied what looked like a log.

"Probably a rotting limb that fell off one of these trees," said Vernon. He looked up to me and grinned. "You want to see?"

I scowled, but placed a mask over my face, and without the tank and fins, slipped into water up to my waist. My bare feet hit a mass of wiggling grass that felt like snakes.

"God's going to get you for this, Vernon Drake!" I took a breath and shoved my face into the water. Up close the object didn't look much like a log or a limb. And it wasn't rotten. I raised my head, took another deep breath and leaned into the water. With both hands I grasped the ends of the nearly two-foot long box, all the while praying it wasn't a home for a water moccasin.

I pulled against the mud that sucked on the metal box. When it finally came to the top, its weight pushed me backward and I sat in the heavy grass.

By the time we got the box and me into the boat, I felt I had been on an hour dive. "Nasty part of the river," I said as I pulled off strands of hydrilla. Tiny frogs jumped from the grass back into the water.

"What the hell is this?" Vernon unsheathed his knife to push at the metal box. It had no rust or dents, only river debris. "Looks like somebody's idea of a tackle box." He shook it slightly. We heard something like the tinkling of glass against glass amid the slosh of water.

"Guess we'll have to let Amado open it," I said. I was tempted, but the lid wouldn't lift with a nudge of the knife. It would take breaking into, and Tony wouldn't like it if he didn't have first crack.

"We'll do another quick glance on the way back," said Vernon as he backed the boat into a space wide enough to turn around. "Looks like a dark cloud forming."

In the distance, thunder rumbled and flashes of lightning moved across the sky. It played tricks on the eyes inside the heavy swamp growth, like broken laser lights that suddenly came and went.

"Any look is going to be cursory in this stuff," I said, anxious to move out of the gathering lightning.

"Like Pasquin says, don't worry. I'll get you to safety."

"Pasquin was born with a rabbit's foot." I leaned over the side to keep my mind off the rumble that didn't sound so distant now. Something shuffled on the shore.

"What's that?" said Vernon as he stared into the trees.

I lifted my eyes to see something dart into the palmetto bushes and stop, then dart again between two tree trunks. The noise rustled through undergrowth. When the lightning flashed again, the white of the movement stood out for a second.

"A deer?" asked Vernon.

"I swear it's a woman," I said and stood in the boat. Thunder pounded the sky. "And I swear she's nude!"

"Better sit down. You'll be the tallest thing on the water, and you know how lightning picks out its subjects." Vernon revved the engine.

When we reached the cove where the skeleton rested on the bottom, we had been drenched again, from above this time. The rain pounded, blocking our view except for a few feet in front. We tied up and dashed for the trailers.

Pasquin sat in the back of Amado's car, waving his hat in front of his face even though Tony had left the engine running and the air conditioning on. "Little rain never hurt you." He laughed as Vernon and I darted past him to the diving trailer.

"There's somebody back in those woods, Pasquin," I said as I paused in the blinding rain. "Your moment is coming."

Inside, we peeled off the wet suits and wrapped ourselves in towels. There was no air conditioning here, and we sat in the humidity, watching the rain make mud holes in the earth just outside the door. Lightning flashed and waved all around us as though electricity was trying to set up a force right in the forest. Thunder pounded, and somewhere not too far away, a loud crack signaled that a tree had been hit. I jumped.

"If it gets us, we'll go together," laughed Vernon and took hold of me. Our bodies, clothed only in bathing suits and pouring sweat from the humid heat, clung in a slippery embrace. Each time the lightning flashed, we squeezed each other automatically until we could barely breathe.

Suddenly it was over. Thunder rumbled in the distance like a mad giant lumbering off to another dimension. The rain slowed to a light shower, then to a mist.

"Hey!" A call came from the area where the crane had been attached to the sunken boat.

We slipped from the trailer and splashed mud on our shins all the way to the river bank. A diver stood on the bank next to Marshall Long. Both pointed into the water.

"I guess we loosened the thing when we attached the pulley." The diver paced the bank.

"Dang thing done come up!" Pasquin shaded his eyes and stared into the water.

"Drake and Fogarty!" shouted Tony who had joined the excitement on the bank. "Get into the water and get that out!"

The river surface was dotted with dwindling raindrops. Underwater grasses waved with the currents and the atmospheric disturbance. In the middle of it all, the white skull bobbed, its eye sockets now clear of mud. It suddenly turned on one side as a ghost swimmer might turn its head to take a breath. On top, it had an extra socket, not one that normally formed in a human being. It had the clear, rounded edges of a bullet hole.

CHAPTER THREE

I swam for the skull, its grinning teeth smiling wider as I approached. With my hands rounded as though I were taking a baby's face in a loving embrace, I gripped the cheek bones and kicked to shore, the skull out front like a guiding light. Vernon had put on his tank and was checking below to make sure no other bones had escaped their watery locker.

"Your evidence," I said as I pushed the skull into Marshall's gloved hands. He stood on the bank, his untied tennis shoes moving unsteadily in the slick mud. His bulky body leaned over and threatened to tumble into the river.

"Gotcha!" He jerked backward with the skull in his hand and nearly landed on his well padded butt. Another tech blocked his fall, making a comment about getting extra pay for that.

Vernon called the all clear and climbed ashore with me.

"Get the crane going now!" Tony called to the deputies from his side of the bank. His crisp shirt and creased pants had begun to collect sweat and tiny black bugs. He knocked them off, refusing to share his clothes with insects. His jaw worked in agitation, a sure sign of impatience with the way things were developing.

The crane operator turned on the ignition and the machine gave a roar. The river gave up its wreckage in a sucking sound that would rival a whale's blow in open seas. When the boat rested at the surface, its bow pointed upward, dragging a stern that was a ragged wreck, the crane reared backward and dragged the whole thing onto

26

the bank.

"Right there!" said Tony. He had moved to the side of the scene tape and held up his hand.

By late afternoon, the techs and the deputies had the boat pieces cleaned of river mud and the skeleton spread out on an evidence bag. Marshall sat in his folding chair and poked around the arm area.

"Needs some more here and a little in the back area. Think you divers can sift the bottom of the river?"

"The others are down there now, Marshall. I've had enough for one day. You push us too far, you'll have more than one skeleton to rearrange." I sipped on the standard sheriff's issue of sweet orange soda that had grown warm.

"We got to make some arrangements," said Tony. "Can't leave this body out here overnight."

"Take a picture and wrap him up," said Marshall.

"Him?" I asked.

"White male, past fifty, I'd say. Bullet through the brain. Other than that, can't tell you anything 'til we do the lab stuff."

As the deputies enclosed the skeleton in a box, the crowd that had gathered on the opposite bank began to murmur, then move back to allow an elderly man to pass through. He wore a long black coat in spite of the sweltering heat.

"You must pray for your iniquities, ask for forgiveness, and hope for redemption!" He yelled in our direction and held up one hand as though reaching for God was the same as *sig-heiling* Hitler.

"Oh, lordy, it's Barley Ben," said Pasquin and moved to a better place to watch the action. "He's going to be all over that skeleton if you let him near us.

"Get him over here," said Tony.

Two deputies who stood on the opposite bank took Barley Ben

by the elbows and put him in a boat. This was his opportunity to recall the River Jordan and its somewhat foggy relationship to behaving one's self on this earth. He sat in the front and "gloried to God" the few yards across the water lane.

"What's your name?" Tony asked, the Barley part not acceptable to official law.

"The earthly name is of no importance. The kingdom to come names us and that is based upon our actions here on this evil earth." He planned to say more, but just then, Marshall lifted the skull off the ground and slipped it into a separate cardboard box. Barley's eyes opened wide.

"Your name, sir?" asked Tony again.

Barley gulped. "Is that real?" His hand reached out to point and began to shake.

"Your name?" Tony's agitation grew and his normal pale olive skin reddened.

"Somebody been eaten?" He kept shaking his finger at the boxed skull. "Gators are taking retribution."

Tony moved closer. A deputy followed and stood close to the man. "Pat him down," said Tony.

Barley Ben leaned both arms against the coroner's wagon as the deputy patted his big coat and the clothes underneath.

"Bible, keys, a pocket knife, and this," said the deputy as he held up a square-shaped liquor bottle. Barley's gaze stayed with the techs who loaded their evidence in the back of the van. His eyes widened each time they slipped in another container.

"There's your barley!" said Pasquin who slapped his thigh with his hat and let out a laugh. "Nothing like good old God's brew and a little preaching."

"He smells like a medicine cabinet," said the deputy who had patted him down. He pulled off the bottle top and sniffed the contents. "Like you said, God's brew."

"It's not against the law," said Tony and handed the bottle to Barley, who immediately unstopped it and took a long swig.

"If I'd known about that…" He jabbed a thumb at the evidence wagon. "God help us." He bowed his head and closed his eyes. His body swayed, and it appeared he would fall into the water. Suddenly his eyes shot open. "Innocence, thou art all too soon corrupted!" He lifted the bottle and gulped down the liquid.

"Indeed, it is!" laughed Pasquin.

If we thought our work was done for the day, Tony let us know our misconception. He ordered Vernon and me to accompany Pasquin into the woods and find out who lived back there. We decided to take the boat again to the end of the creek and go ashore there.

"Might be a house or two along the way," said Pasquin. He sat in the front and fanned himself as we moved slowly down the water lane.

The sun had returned with a vengeance, mixing with the moisture from the heavy rain, and creating a wet blanket effect, the electric kind on full blast. Vernon and I had pulled on jeans and tee shirts over our suits.

"Let's hurry and get under the tree canopy, please," I said as I swatted at a horse fly that buzzed my damp hair.

"Keep an eye out for shacks or any sign of life on shore," said Vernon as he guided the boat into the narrow watery passage. He had placed a sheriff's department cap over his bald pate and dark glasses on his tanned face. The hard muscles of his arms flexed as he turned the boat. The only thing missing was his wide grin that melted me faster than a popsicle in Florida heat.

"Seems I recall a fellow living not too far from the end of this creek," said Pasquin. He had been watching me look at Vernon. He grinned and nodded as though he knew exactly what I was thinking.

"Who?" I said, and turned my face away from him.

"Old man—older than me." He laughed and it echoed into the forest. "Used to live in a trailer until the thing rusted out. Think he put up a cement block place."

We came to the end of the creek. Vernon tossed the rope ashore and stepped into the water. "You'll have to wade again, Luanne." He grinned now, and somewhere in my psyche I said "finally, a smile."

"Just pull on the boat 'til the bow scrapes shore," said Pasquin. "We won't have to get too wet."

This old man knew the river like he knew himself. His rhythms and the river's had long ago made harmony. When the currents changed, Pasquin changed with them. His topknot of white hair stood to attention each time he pulled off his straw hat. Underneath, a time worn leathery skin made him look akin to some of his fellow swamp creatures.

Vernon tied the rope around a young tree and steadied the boat as we stepped off and into grassy mud that threatened to bog us down. After moving away from the marshy area, Pasquin stopped and rubbed his muddy shoes against a tree trunk. He bent his head over, pointing his white hair downward like some divining rod.

"That way," he said. His ancient body moved under the low hanging branches of oak trees. "Watch that oak snake." Pasquin pointed to the fork in a tree at least as old as he. The brown and black spotted snake must have been four feet long. It moved around the fat trunk and headed away from us. Nonpoisonous, it was more interested in critters of the trees.

"Anybody hear a rattle, stop dead," I said.

"Most likely hear one, too," said Pasquin. "This is their territory."

I shivered. In spite of living all my life in this terrain, I had not conquered the fear of snakes. Even coming face to face with one wouldn't make me kill it. I just feared it, froze until my blood pressure dropped. I could bash a man's head in with a shovel, but not a snake's. The idea that I held one end of a weapon and touched the snake with the other was too much connection with primitive forces.

After a walk that seemed to take us in circles, Pasquin made a gesture as though presenting us to Paradise. In fact, that's what it said in crude writing over the moldy cement block structure: PARADISE.

"Guess it is to a hermit," Vernon said. We stood before it as though waiting for St. Peter to unlock the gates.

Pasquin rapped at the door for a minute, but then announced himself the Cajun way with a "whooooeee!" and marched around one side of the building. Vernon and I stood still.

The forest went silent. Even Pasquin's rustling footsteps disappeared. After a few seconds, Vernon and I looked at each other. He nodded and I followed. Before getting half way round, Pasquin was headed back, a man of his own generation following a few yards behind, and, like Pasquin, sporting a thick head of white hair.

"Been trying to grow sweet potatoes in this soil," said the man who leaned a hoe against the side of the cement block.

"This here's Jacob Halley. Been living in and out of this swamp 'bout long as me." Pasquin tipped his hat toward the man who brushed off his hands on a long sleeved blue shirt.

"Sorry, been piddlin' in the dirt," he said and grinned to show the presence of four natural teeth on his bottom gum.

"Are you aware of a missing teenager on the river?" asked Vernon after showing his badge.

Jacob shook his head and closed his nearly toothless mouth. "Sad thing, but them kids and their fast boats…" He went silent and continued to shake his head.

"What about the boats sunk in the creek down here?"

Jacob grunted recognition. "Them things! People seem to think this is graveyard creek. Leave old boats on the shore 'til they rot and eventually get pulled into the water by high tide and sunk. Damn nuisance! Was a time when I had to be real careful putting in my own boat down there. Don't do it anymore. Got a spot up near the river. I just walk to the boat." Jacob scratched his stomach.

"Anybody else live around here?" said Pasquin who strode a few steps away from the house.

"Plenty, but don't come around here much. I like it that way." Jacob laughed. "But I can give ya'll something cold to drink."

We followed him inside the ugly gray blocks where it was cool without air conditioning, but damp with the odor of swamp dirt. He had tiled the floor in bright blue vinyl and attached simulated wood paneling to the walls. One tiny room housed a couch and chair at one end, a dinette set at the other. He motioned us to sit and disappeared into a narrow dark hall.

Vernon took his time before sitting down. He followed his deputy training by looking over the room thoroughly. Pasquin took the chair next to a large crate that served as a side table.

"No television?" I said.

"Too noisy," said Jacob as he returned with four cans of cola, the tops popped. "Got one stored in the shed. Want to buy it?"

I smiled and changed the subject. "Is there a woman who lives around here?"

"Couple guys who fish here got wives. They're on down the swamp a bit, closer to Scrapper Creek." Jacob sipped loudly on his can. Condensed moisture dripped down his fingers and onto his sleeve.

"What about kids skinny-dipping in the water?"

"What? Ain't nobody going to swim in that nasty water." Jacob laughed. "Kids maybe push each other in sometimes, but that's up on the river, never down here."

We continued to sip in silence. If Jacob knew anything, he wasn't saying. I placed my drink on the vinyl floor. "Do you mind if I use your restroom?"

Jacob pointed a finger down the dark hall. "Just there. Straight back and you'll find it."

Halfway down the hall, I noticed a door that led into a tiny kitchen. Its refrigerator and stove seemed out of a ship's galley, a small ship. One clean cup and saucer sat on the drain board. Jacob had a view of his swamp out of a tiny window about shoulder high.

Across the hall a few steps away, another door led to his sleeping quarters. It had a cot, made up neatly, and a portable clothes rack at the other end. A book shelf with a table lamp in the shape of a dock post served as a bedside stand. A radio sat beside the lamp. A couple of books rested atop stacks of magazines on the shelves, all in fine order.

The bathroom, clean and tiny, followed the rest of this make-shift abode. One end had a toilet and sink that sat beneath a high square window. The other end was an open shower. He had made the floor slant down slightly here, so that water would pour into the drain and not into the toilet side. One long rack held two towels and a wash cloth. The floor had none of the tale-tell sand that often plagued swamp dweller's homes. I closed the door, noticing the air freshening spray atop the toilet tank. These old eccentrics like order in their lives, I thought. That's why they live out here where they see nature as a pattern. A television or inebriated kids doing shark circles in a speed boat would be an upset to their universes. I flushed the toilet, moved into the hallway and back to the others.

"Anybody go missing around here in the past year?" Vernon was leaning forward on the sofa, gripping the soda can.

"Don't keep track if they did," said Jacob. "I didn't move out here to notice other's coming and going, unless they come on my space." He grinned. "You find everything all right, miss?"

I nodded and sat down with Vernon. The cheap sofa was covered in green vinyl, but it had none of the stains its age should have commanded. Like the rest of the house, Jacob kept it spotless, although without decorative cushions.

"You got the time to show us around, say between here and Scrapper Creek?" Pasquin dipped his soda in a kind of salute.

"Shore! I ain't having no fun growing taters anyhow." Jacob stood and grabbed a cloth hat as battered as pasquin's straw one. "You got to walk. I ain't got one of them swamp buggies."

"You ever see swamp buggies back here?" said Vernon. He handed over his can to Jacob who gathered the others and carried them to the kitchen.

"Once in a while. Not too good back here. Lots of brush and stuff. Man! Them things are noisy."

"Where're we headed?" asked Pasquin.

"Might as well follow the path," he said. "Man lives right up that lane with his cat. Funny college fellow. Won't eat meat and gets annoyed by people."

"How does he live?" I asked.

Jacob looked my way and winked. This man wasn't taking me seriously. Pasquin noticed and winked at me, too.

"Something in government research, he says. Got all this equipment inside a trailer."

CHAPTER FOUR

The vegetarian man with a cat turned out to be a graduate student doing summer research on soil and water pollution. Sam Nettleson sat on the narrow step of his trailer, moving vials from a box to a lab carrier. He stood up suddenly when we approached.

"Sorry I can't ask you inside. It's not quite big enough for me much less three other people." He rubbed a palm across his shorts and stuck it out. He wore battered sandals and pulled his stringy brown hair into a pony tail.

Vernon asked the same questions he had asked Jacob, all the while taking in the scene of the trailer inside a closed swamp area.

"How did you get this trailer in here?" I said.

"Didn't. Somebody told me about it and figured I could rent it for the summer. It's been here a while, but serves my purpose for now." He turned his gaunt face, a carbon copy of a sixties hippie, and smiled at me. "You wouldn't want it for a summer home."

"Who owns it?" asked Vernon.

"Got it through a management company in Tallahassee. You'll have to ask them who the owner is."

Sam Nettleson knew nothing of the missing teen, nor of a nude woman in the woods. "There is a crazy old broad who comes off the creek sometimes and hikes through here. Don't think she's ever stripped or streaked." Sam sniggered at his own humor.

"Crazy Alice!" said Jacob who had squatted against a tree trunk. "I forgot about her. She don't live in the swamp, not far as I know anyhow. She's got a small boat and does odd jobs for people around here. Cleans my place every once in a while."

"You see her buck naked?" Pasquin had a hard time keeping his face serious.

Jacob wasn't so successful. He burst into laughter, "Lordy! I hope not!"

"Look, I don't know if this has anything to do with whatever you're looking for, but I've had several things go missing around here." Sam waved toward the trailer. "I lock the place but it's not much of a deterrent. And lots of times I'm just down there and don't even shut the door." He pointed to a stream that ran into Scrapper Creek.

"What kind of things?" said Vernon.

"Equipment. Boxes and jars."

"No food or guns?"

"I have no gun, but I do have some fishing rods. Nobody took those." Sam opened the door to the tiny trailer and leaned his upper body inside. He pulled something toward him. "I've lost four of these." He held up a metal box.

"I think I know where one is," said Vernon. He took the box and opened it. "Lab vials?" He held up one of the stoppered vials.

"I store the samples I collect in these boxes. Got one entire box filled and then it disappeared. You think somebody is taking them for tackle boxes?" Sam closed the door.

Before anyone could answer, a rustle and a giggle moved from around the trailer. A woman whose gray hair stroked her waist trotted up to Sam and grabbed his arm. "Got me a man!" She tossed her head back and laughed.

"I'm not your man, Alice," said Sam. He winced and tried to pull away from the woman. Her loose muu-muu caught on his belt. "Let go."

Alice's faded blue eyes opened wide and stared at us. Still smiling, she repeated, "I got me a man!"

"That's nice," I said and took Vernon's arm. "I've got one, too."

Alice's smile suddenly faded and confusion spread over the lines in her forehead. Then she grinned again and said, "Mine's younger."

That broke the uneasiness. We all laughed until Jacob asked her about her cleaning day.

"Be there Friday—if my man don't mind." She broke into a loud holler this time, revealing solid white teeth. She lifted the hem of her muu-muu and did a little dance with one foot. Her ragged sandals were a match for Sam Nettleson's.

Vernon shrugged and moved toward the woman. "You hear anything about the kid who fell overboard last night?"

Alice's face lost the smile. She cocked her head as though listening for an echo somewhere in the forest. She began to shake her head. "Got to go," she whispered. "Got a job at the Ocean Pine." She turned and ran into the woods as quietly as she had come.

"She's not talking about the Ocean Pine Cafe down on the bay?" said Vernon.

"Yeah. She does some kind of cleaning up for them, not in the restaurant itself but in that little motel they run alongside it." Jacob grunted as he stood up. "She ain't a bad sort and she cleans like nobody's business. Always shows up, too. She's just a little 'techted' in the noggin." He yanked off his hat and pointed to his head.

We moved around Sam's trailer. He had a table set up in back, but no vials or tubes or boxes sat here. It was a sort of "half-way station," where he got his samples in order before stowing them inside, he said.

"Miracle this old thing doesn't leak," he said, pointing to the trailer. "Got rust all around the outside." He shoved aside some debris that looked like hydrilla grass cut in small sections. "Can't store anything out here. Rains too much."

"Have many visitors?" asked Vernon who eyed the back door of the trailer. It was padlocked from the outside.

"None. The university expects me to keep notes and write up all my results in the Fall, but they don't care what goes on down here. Just so long as I don't go over the grant budget." He noticed Vernon's gaze. "I had to use a padlock on that door. The normal lock is gone and the handle on the inside fell off. I rigged up the clasp. It's not much. Anybody could jerk it off with one strong pull, but it'd make a hell of a noise."

"Not the most secure place you live in," said Vernon. "Hope you don't smoke. This place could go up fast."

"Don't smoke or cook. The only thing I got inside is a tiny refrigerator and lights." He pointed to the overhead wire coming off a pole the electric company had set up years back. "Eating has become a raw vegetable and fruit activity with an occasional granola bar."

From the looks of Sam's thin body, he indeed wasn't getting his ration of fried fish and hushpuppies, not to mention pecan pie. He didn't seem to care.

Sam pointed to two lanes that forked away from his place. One led to the shore of Scrapper Creek, the other into the forest and presumably on to other trailers and cabins of swamp dwellers.

"Haven't met anybody else, just Alice and Jacob." He smiled at Halley.

"You have a cell phone?" I asked.

He pulled the tiny instrument from his shorts pocket. "My line to the world."

Scrapper Creek was at low tide when we reached it by foot. No boat could navigate it now without scraping bottom, and a swimmer would find himself entangled in a mass of grass. We stood on

the bank and watched a three-foot alligator climb onto the opposite shore, find him a spot in the setting sun, and come to a dead
stop. In the distance, an owl awoke and began his "who-who" song.
It wouldn't be long before the frogs would congregate near the
water and make a noise that many have called the "all night sing."

"We'll come back tomorrow and put in a boat here," said Vernon.

Jacob and Pasquin fanned themselves with their hats. I used my
hands to sweep away the faint, darting mosquitoes who needed
blood for their babies. I had a particularly bad itch from some big
bite I'd received earlier. Stooping to the edge of the creek, I tried to
reach enough water for a hand scoop. Just as I was about to stick
my hand down into the grass, a thick brown stick moved through
the water. I fell backwards.

"Moccasin!" I felt lucky to have only an itch.

Pasquin and Vernon teased me all the way back to Jacob's place.
"Some swamp woman you are. Scared of a snake that was scared
of you." Pasquin didn't let up. "Should stay home and have a bunch
of babies." He chuckled knowing that suggestion had always annoyed me. I was in my late forties now and had no intention of
having babies whether I stayed home or not.

Vernon's addition to the taunting was to grab a blade of grass
and use it to tickle my neck. I slapped at it like it was a mosquito. He
just tucked the grass behind his ear and pulled the same trick a few
steps later.

We stood in front of Jacob's house. He had been a quiet partici-
pant in our walk, and I just realized that he hadn't laughed at the
boyish pranks and chauvinistic remarks.

"Don't let these two get at you, ma'am. Snakes are nothing to
joke about. I got proof." He pulled up a sleeve to show a nasty scar
that resembled an old burn on the inside of his forearm. "Moccasin got me there from reaching into the water just like you did.

Only I didn't see him 'swimming away from me.' I figured he was lying in wait."

"When did that happen?" asked Pasquin.

"Couple of years back. I got the bright idea of putting some beer cans in the creek to cool them down. I might have died from this thing if Alice hadn't come along. She got all upset about me fiddling around in the water like that. But she shoved me in a boat and got me to the river where an ambulance came. Damn!—pardon me, ma'am—but this arm was black and swollen big as Popeye's arm." He held it up now, like a trophy of a life-death game he had played.

"Alice knows boats, then?" I asked.

"Woman knows lots of things. Don't let that addle brain act fool you." Jacob tipped his hat and looked at the sky. "Ya'll better get going. Night coming soon."

CHAPTER FIVE

And night arrived with a summer wind and thunder clap that rivaled an army invasion. Lightning flickered across the sky like so many space lasers at intervals of less than ten seconds. It would last for hours, startling with glaring flashes, then pounding roof tops with a burst of thunder. It acted like labor pains where the baby, in this case the rain, would not budge. A dry electrical storm, primitive yet futuristic, it evoked human fears like nothing else.

I wrapped myself in a sofa throw, sat cross-legged in the middle of the floor and prayed the current wouldn't cut off. But the weather gods had other ideas. The air conditioning shut down, and the table lamps went dark. I wasn't cold and would even be sweltering in half an hour, but the throw gave me comfort. I felt like an Indian in a teepee as flashes and glares flew about me for hours. Even with the curtains closed, the light shimmied through the living room.

Sometime in the drama of the night, I heard a familiar scratching on the door. My swamp dog, Plato, had forsaken his jaunt into the forest and was seeking the safety of home.

"Get in here, you mutt!" I opened the door just as a slam of lightning lit up the entire yard like a flash bulb from hell. Plato gave a little screech, tucked his tail, and scooted inside. "Where have you been?" He wagged the tail a couple of times, but the flashing lights disturbed him and he headed behind a chair. Curling up, he shook a little, then shoved his nose under the chair to shade his eyes. "Some fierce guard dog you are," I said and sat down beside him. We were two animals, the prehistoric parts of our brains working overtime and wishing for the demons to stop their skylight bickering.

It seemed an eternity that the psychedelia flashed around us, the drumming and banging of thunder so loud I barely heard the knock on the door. It was only ten o'clock.

Plato whimpered and scooted into the center of the room on his stomach, not knowing whether to attack the person at the door or hide from the lightning. I waited for a flash to light up the porch, then looked through the peep hole.

"Harry?" I opened the front door to see the salt and pepper hair surrounded by an aura from the sky. He leaned on a walking stick.

"You got time to talk to me, Luanne?" His face would have that hang-dog look if I could see it. He hated asking for help, but he had done it in the past. Then he had asked me to dive with him.

Inside, he let himself sit hard on the sofa. Plato did his sniffing job then retreated to the back of the chair. I sat across from Harry, the lightning flashes revealing us to each other every few seconds.

"I've got all the time in the world, Harry. Nature has decided I don't need electric current for light and cooling." I leaned toward him, but stopped when I realized it was not a gesture we shared. Instead, I lit a candle on the table. "What's up?"

Thunder clapped hard, shaking the room. Plato appeared at my ankles, whimpering and pleading for the whole thing to stop. I rubbed his head and said soothing things.

"I guess I need some of that," said Harry.

"Petting? You'll have to find some other woman, Harry."

"I mean care—diving care. You know what's wrong with me, don't you?"

"Scared shitless to go into the caves again?" He couldn't see my face, but I could sense his giving in to reality.

"I want some help there, Luanne. Can't live like this. The leg doesn't hamper swimming. It's just that when I get near a cave open-ing, my first inclination is to check the sides for devices."

"Nothing wrong with that, especially since you do so much po-lice work."

"Yeah, well, even though I never find anything, the idea of en-tering into that hole freezes me right up. I can feel my heart pound-ing and the breathing getting unsteady." He sat silent, letting Mother Nature do all the complaining.

"And what can I do that some psychiatrist can't?" I scratched Plato's ears. He moved to a belly position, his chin resting on my toes.

"Do practice dives with me. Out here at your landing. Gradually get me back into a cave."

"And suppose I don't succeed?"

He sighed and shrugged his shoulders. "It will be me who doesn't succeed. But if there is a chance, you're it, Luanne." He looked at me through the darkness. The lightning flashes had diminished and begun to move away from the area. The candle provided most of the light now.

"I don't know, Harry." I leaned back on the sofa. Plato had lifted his head and seemed like a dog again. The thoughts of seeing Harry every day, swimming with him, even consoling him when he couldn't make the dive, led me into territory I long avoided.

"You're not teaching this summer, right?"

I wasn't. My job as professor of linguistics at the university fi-nally gave me a summer off. The relief of not having to repeat courses I had taught for years and grading the papers to go with them left me near giddy at the end of the spring semester.

"We could go out twice a week, maybe?" Harry sounded plead-ing, whiny, as though he needed an ear scratching.

Plato braved up and stood and sniffed the air. He wagged his tail and went to Harry. Harry pet him in greeting and the two bonded in friendliness.

"I wouldn't interfere with your other work, and certainly not with…you know."

I nodded. He meant Vernon, my lover, confidant, and diving companion who never stood in my way. Jealousy wasn't something he revealed to the world, not even to me. Maybe he wasn't. But because he had never shown any kind of possessiveness didn't mean that I wanted to flaunt it in his face. It wasn't Vernon I mistrusted. It was myself.

"When do you want to start?" I asked and the answer came with the last of flickering sky lights.

"This week?"

Harry's eyes appeared to water a bit as he left my front porch. The electricity back on, the dim light reflected the embarrassment at having to go to a female, a former lover—one he had betrayed for some young grad student, at that—to help him back into cave diving. We agreed to work around Tony's case, to swim when Vernon was on duty.

My sense of guilt multiplied as I watched the taillights on Harry's car disappear down the rutted road until they became like space invaders bobbing unevenly through the trees. "I'm not responsible for Harry MacAllister," I said aloud. "Why did I say I'd do this?"

Plato looked up at me as though he could answer. "I wish you could, old dog." I scratched his head and went back inside the stuffy living room. It would take a while for the air conditioner to recool the house. Plato, with little remembrance of his fear of lightning, pushed against the screen and let himself into the dark swamp. "Take care, hound dog," I whispered as he faded into the dark.

I felt abandoned, no dog, no Harry, Vernon on duty, and sleep wouldn't come. I lay in my renovated bedroom on a bed with a new

mattress and clean curtains on the windows. It would be nothing
like the cots Sam Nettleson and Jacob would sleep on tonight. But
then losing electricity for a couple of hours may not faze either
man.

Swamp life had a closeness about it. The very air, humid and
constantly warm, surrounded you with close-ups of insect sounds.
If you were anywhere near water, frogs could send up a croaking
that crescendoed with the passing night. Mosquitoes and "no-
seeums" flitted about, taking bites out of sweaty skin, leaving an
itch that confounded sleep. My eyes finally closed, and I dreamed
of Alice running through the bushes and trees, her long gray hair
blending with the strands of moss that whisked her naked body.

Morning brought Vernon, a welcome sight after my encounter with
the off-balance Harry. In spite of a nervousness of having to tell
him about the upcoming activity between Harry and me, I wanted
Vernon to be there, to steady the forces as he had done for nearly
three years now. He stood on the porch, grinning that boyish way
that suckered me right into his realm.

"We need to meet with Amado and Mr. Hanover. Seems the
man is really on a tear about his kid not being found. He's demand-
ing to question the divers and anyone else who searched." He mussed
my hair that hadn't been combed yet. "Get dressed."

While I showered and dressed, Vernon sat on the porch, his feet
resting on the screen boards. It was early morning when you could
enjoy the outdoors in steamy Florida weather. After ten, it would
be too humid.

When I emerged from the living room, Pasquin had joined
Vernon. The two were droning on about water pollution and encroaching tourists.

"Never saw so many swimmers down to the Springs," said Pasquin. "Too many bodies anywhere is going to dirty up the stream." He fanned with his straw hat, a vintage piece that threatened to break off at the ends any minute.

"State has too many people," said Vernon. "This end of it isn't used to the crowds."

"Prices are right," I said as I joined the men. I passed around glasses of orange juice.

"Won't be for long," said Vernon. "Somebody gave me an offer on my place. Couldn't believe my ears."

I glanced his way. A tiny dart of worry coursed through me. Why would Vernon entertain offers on his place?

"Won't be selling until I'm an old coot who can't walk down the river lane anymore." He smiled at Pasquin.

"If you live like this one, you won't ever sell," I said, shooting him a questioning look. "Pasquin walks down river lanes and swamp lanes and just about any other kind."

"Ma'am," he said in his characteristic tease, "you saying that I'm an old coot?"

"Not hardly." I sipped my juice. "What are you doing out so early anyway?" Pasquin had kept the old Cajun habits of staying up late, drinking and singing with his swamp buddies. He tended to grouch around for hours if someone roused him too early.

"Your sheriff man done woke me up. Said I was to come along with Miz Fogarty." He saluted me with the orange juice glass then drank the last in one gulp.

"Amado has his days," I said. "Maybe we'd best be going."

Vernon drove us in his patrol car down the narrow dirt lane towards the paved road. The ruts were uneven and wild shrubs brushed against the sides of the car. It was time to call in the road scrapers, something I tried to do every summer.

"Nearly lost my hat," Pasquin said after one rather hard bump on the trail. "You done spring cleaning yet?"

Amado stood with his hands on his hips at the search site. Other cops leaned against the cars and stared into the forest. The man I had seen the first day of diving, Tommy Hanover's father, paced near the edge of the river. From a distance, he was a tall, striking figure with close-cropped gray hair.

Amado spied our car and hurried to meet us. "The man is in a real piss over this. Thinks we can magically locate his son and wants to know why we haven't. He's used to bossing people around." He turned to see Hanover approaching the car, a stern frown sending out "dare me" signals.

After brief introductions, Hanover stood firmly in his expensive running suit, his legs slightly parted like some heroic statue and his arms hanging stiffly at his side. I got the impression of someone ready to ball up a fist and clobber the first face that came near.

"I want to know just what has been done to find my son." He stared at us after jerking off his sunshades. His eyes, blue and bloodshot, stared from a face full of rage. He was tan and showed signs of daily workouts. It was obvious that he enjoyed his money, took the things it had to offer, including high-priced liquor. He slammed the glasses back over his eyes.

Tony sighed and faced the man. They were near the same height and they matched scowls, Tony's black eyes attempting to stare down Hanover's blue ones.

"We've done all we can," said Tony. "The divers have tracked the currents. More divers are going down today. We got deputies searching the banks."

"It's not enough!" Hanover started to argue but stopped when another car drove up and two teenage girls emerged. The one driving wore the latest tank top and low-hanging pants. When she turned to retrieve her purse from the seat, the pants slid down and a flower tattoo appeared above the tail bone. She had long straight hair. When she turned around again, the ring in her navel shined in the sunlight. Her friend, a shorter version, sported two ponytails out the sides of her head while the rest of her long hair hung down to her waist. Her halter top and low-cut pants revealed the same navel ring. I wondered what sweet little drawing was tattooed on her butt.

"You said we should come here?" The first girl said to Tony.

"These are the two girls who were on the boat with Tommy. Lucky for both they were able to swim ashore when the boat tipped." Tony spoke to us. The girls half smiled, not quite sure of their celebrity status. When they glanced toward Hanover, they stopped smiling and looked to their feet.

"Tell me what happened," said Vernon.

"Already did that," whined the shorter girl.

"Tell me. You see we know about currents and ways of the water. Maybe there's something the others missed."

The girls looked at each other.

"Tell them, damn it!" Hanover made a move toward them. "My only son is out there somewhere. Now speak up!"

Pasquin leaned against Vernon's car and fanned himself. He appeared just an old man listening to the conversation, but his eyes never left Hanover.

"We were going fast and hit something…."

"No, no," said Vernon. "Start at the beginning. What were you doing before you got on the boat."

A tiny giggle escaped from the shorter girl. The tall one shot her a glance. "We were at Tommy's house. On the deck, just hanging."

"Hanging? Define that, uh, your name is?"

"Roxanna," said the tall one, her eyes flitting up in a flirt. "This is Patsy." She nodded toward her friend without removing her gaze from Vernon.

"Go on," said Vernon. He shifted as though he knew they were scrutinizing him.

The girls glanced at each other and stifled giggles again. Tony looked sour but Hanover was ready to kill.

"Get on with it!" he screamed.

"It's just talking, listening to music, dancing a little," said Roxanna. Her eyes lowered then darted up again.

"Drinking and drugging some, too?" said Vernon.

"That's irrelevant," said Hanover, his anger turning from the girls.

"Sir," Tony stepped in, "it's about as relevant as can be. What your son was doing in that boat shows signs of irresponsibility. Now was that caused by just being a teenager and having raging hormones or maybe a little substance helped it along?"

"We had a little rum," said the tall girl.

"Straight from the bottle," Patsy added and smiled. She quickly placed a hand over her mouth.

"Any pills?" Vernon asked.

"Well," Roxanna squirmed.

The group stood silent until Hanover could hold it no longer.

"My son is missing, maybe dead, what's the problem here?" His bellowing voice sounded through the forest. The tall girl jumped.

"Tommy said he had some ecstasy. We took it, but I don't think it was the real stuff because it didn't do anything." She glanced at Hanover then at Tony. "Tommy finally said let's go for a boat ride."

"Did he take ecstasy pills, too?"

The short girl nodded. "And drank the rum."

"Would you say he was drunk?" asked Vernon.

"Now just one minute…" Hanover moved toward Vernon.

Vernon stood tall, a good three inches above the man.

"Alcohol can make a difference in what your son was able to do in the way of saving himself, sir."

Hanover backed away.

"We were all a little high," said the tall girl and shook her hair as if to say it was her privilege to get that way. "But not sot drunk."

"All right, now tell us about the ride and the hit." Vernon turned to the girls again.

The short Patsy shrugged. "We got into the boat. It was tied right there at Tommy's deck. And he raced down the river a little ways and back again. Then he started laughing and speeded up and began going in big circles."

"He called it going round the world," Roxanna added.

"Nearly made me sick," Patsy wanted to giggle again.

"Then the boat just went crunch against something," said the tall girl. "It got out of control, like Tommy was jerking the wheel back and forth and going so fast. It kind of tipped and I just flew into the water."

The short girl nodded, her eyes wide now with the seriousness of the situation.

"Did either of you see Tommy?" I asked.

Both girls shook their heads. Patsy said, "I didn't even see her until I got to shore. I think I remember seeing the boat up against a tree, but Tommy wasn't around."

"Did you see the manatee?" asked Vernon.

"No. We didn't know what happened until somebody said that's what we hit." Roxanna shrugged and pushed against her hair.

I moved to the distraught father. "Mr. Hanover, we traced the currents. Depending on where he landed in the water, he could have been washed toward the bay or rammed against the banks. But we've searched everywhere and there is no sign. Not even a piece of clothing. If he crawled ashore somewhere, we'll find signs."

I waited for the man's face to calm somewhat. "How well does he know the area? I mean the banks, the water, the other houses?"

"He knows the people who live near us, at least has an acquaintance with them. I don't think he's ever explored the river banks here. Just played with that damn boat."

Behind me, I heard Pasquin's whisper, "and with those girls and a few drugs. Bet he's even smoked a joint or two."

Tony passed his cards around to the girls and Hanover and said if they heard anything else to call. He agreed with the father that the search would continue. I followed the girls to their car and leaned inside.

"How did you girls get along with Daddy Hanover," I asked. They both giggled at the name.

"He likes to look," said Patsy. "Especially at belly buttons."

"He really didn't have much to do with us, or his son," said Roxanna as she pushed the key into the ignition. "Tommy got just about all he wanted." She looked up at me with the mature gaze of a seasoned man hunter. "And what he wanted, we wanted."

I stood back and watched their car disappear down the wooded road. Two girls in search of a free ride, it seemed to me.

When Hanover finally got into his SUV, Tony turned to us.

"He's threatened to sue, you know. Sue us for some dumb mistake his kid made."

"He doesn't have a case," I said.

"What's the worst scenario for us?" He asked.

The three of us looked at each other. I said, "I suppose it would be that Tommy got knocked out of the boat, swept a little toward the less-traveled lanes, and got picked off by a hungry gator."

We stood in silence until Tony said, "Jesus, Luanne."

CHAPTER SIX

Pasquin said, "You know what galls me about them two little girls?"
He sat across from me at Mama's Table, the best known fish cafe
on the Palmetto River, and stirred a fried shrimp through some hot
sauce. "They don't have any kind of remorse or sadness about this.
Most they was afraid of was getting yelled at by the kid's father.
Now, back when, they would have been weeping and wailing and
worried sick that their friend was missing, most likely dead."

"Maybe he wasn't so much a friend as a meal ticket. If you see
booze, boats, and drugs as a meal," I said. I tore off part of a
grouper filet and stuffed it in my mouth. The warm cornmeal bat-
ter just barely covered the white flesh.

"You going back into the water?" Pasquin dumped tobasco into
his cheese grits and stirred them to a yellow-red mixture. I winced.

"If Amado says we must, but he's got some other divers working on the search. You want to travel back into the swamp today?"
I picked at my cheese grits. "Vernon is busy but you and I could stir
up some bushes."

"Trouble more like it," he grinned. "You going to eat your hush
puppies?" He didn't wait for an answer but stabbed the fried cornmeal breads with his fork.

Mama, her peroxided locks beginning to show dark roots, joined
us and poured iced tea into tall glasses.

"Old man, you done messed up those grits big time." She made
a face at the tobasco red mixed into the white grits.

Pasquin grinned and nodded. He patted Mama's hand and asked a question completely off the topic of ruination of Southern grits.

"You acquainted with the owners of the Ocean Pine over by the bridge?"

"Couple about to face hard times," Mama said. She grabbed a glass and poured herself some tea. "He's sickly, and she can't manage all the cooking and the motel. I hear they're going to have to sell out. Been laying off help." She waved a hand in the direction of a busboy who loaded up platters of cast-off shrimp shells. "Calvin is the youngest of their boys. First time I ever knew one of them to seek employment outside their own place."

"What about Alice. You know the swamp woman who cleans for them?" Pasquin showed no signs of intense curiosity. Instead, he dipped a spoon into the grits and then rolled them around in his mouth.

"Crazy Alice? They fired her ages ago. She got to hanging around the motel guests instead of cleaning the rooms. Some stuff went missing, and the owners had to replace it."

"What kind of stuff?" I asked.

Mama shrugged. "I hear tell it was men's shirts, and a blanket or two from the motel itself." She took a long swig of her tea. Her hefty frame moved like a graceful dancer between the close set tables. "Woman is nuts. I hear she's took to wearing no clothes on hot days." She laughed at her own comment and strode into the kitchen.

"How does a woman like that live?" I asked as I made a pyramid by stacking hush puppies in my plate.

"Her old Pa left her a trust, I hear tell. Gets cash from that and sold off the land where she grew up." Pasquin scraped the bottom of the grits bowl, making chalkboard sounds that sent chills up my spine.

"And Jacob. He makes a living out of that patch?"

"Nah! He's a vet. Gets some kind of pension off that. Used to work, too. Bet he's got some social security." Pasquin started to take a sip of tea then did a double take. "Looky there! Barley Ben done come in."

He wasn't easy to miss. In spite of having the entryway all to himself, the man bumped both sides of the door jamb before tripping into the cafe. He held one hand on his forehead as he sat hard on a booth bench. Mama moved her ample hips between the tables and stood over the man.

"Been on a binge, again?" She motioned for the busboy to bring a cup of coffee. "Or maybe you've been preaching too hard."

"Done lost my religion, Mama," he said and leaned heavily on the back of the booth. "My head is falling off, and I'm gonna shake to death. You got any wine?"

Mama nodded to the bus boy, motioning him to head back to the kitchen. He came running out again with a glass and an unlabeled wine bottle.

"Just for the shakes, Ben. Then you got to eat and get on out of here." She poured a half glass of something that could have been vodka. "You smell today. Washed lately?"

Barley Ben grasped the glass with both hands and lifted the liquid to his mouth. He sucked in the liquor and swallowed hard. Looking down at the remaining libation in his glass, he upturned it again and finished off his medicine.

"Now," he said. "Now, now, now." He finally looked up at Mama and smiled. "Now, can I have some fried grouper tails?"

Mama shrugged, grabbed the bottle and headed off to the kitchen. She stopped abruptly, turned back to the man and pointed a finger at him. "Don't you go preaching in here, Old Man!"

Barley Ben saluted her. While he waited, he seemed to realize he was in a public place and began to look around. Spying Pasquin and me, he saluted again. "Just spent some hours talking to the sheriff," he said. "Nasty business down on the river." He smiled briefly, then turned his face to the window. He frowned and appeared deep in concentration on some demon that had popped to the edge of his mind.

Hush puppies and grits consumed, Pasquin and I left Mama's Table for the dock where he tied his boat. An old man who couldn't guide a car down a road if he tried, Pasquin revved up the motor and guided it with youthful precision between the other boats into the open river. A still mugginess rested on the surface, sending up swamp mud odors. Clusters of black insects swarmed, put aside only by the flow of air as we sped, Pasquin-style, down the river toward the brackish water. It was a long ride, one that took us past overhanging oaks that dipped their branches into clear cold water, where gators climbed ashore to soak their reptilian blood in the hot sun.

A family of turtles, in graduating sizes, sat in a line on top of a fallen oak limb. A crane raised his long front leg out of the water and in again, his lengthy beak poking about the shallows for minnows. It was truly a lazy river, a peaceable kingdom. Until our motor rocked the universe. The turtles went first, over the side of the branch. The crane took flight, its wide, white wingspread sailing into the sky. The gator was the last. Its moment in the sun disturbed by the vibration, it turned and slipped into the deep.

"Almost to Scrapper Creek," said Pasquin. I had dozed off and on, glimpsing the action of wildlife only half-heartedly.

"You know where to tie up?" I leaned over and ran my hand through the cold water, then splashed it against my face.

"Only one place to do that." Pasquin slowed at the manatee warning signs and eased past wood frame cabins that locals used for weekends of fishing, places where living with critters and mud dirt was okay because you were on the river. "Sign up there." He pointed to a wide opening. Someone had stuck a homemade sign with "Scrapper Creek" scrawled across it.

We headed into a water lane, wide at first but narrowing until we reached a battered landing. A fisherman, his day-old beard and grimy khakis revealing a habit of early morning jaunts, was just untying and heading back to the river.

"Mornin'," he tipped his baseball cap. "Fish ain't bitin' today, folks." He didn't wait for an answer, but revved his engine slightly and eased into the wider areas.

"Lots of people out here these days," said Pasquin. "Somebody's bound to see that kid floating about sooner or later."

"If he's not entangled in some underwater debris," I said.

"You would have found him by now, ma'am," Pasquin said, in an attempt to console me and the other divers. "He'll get found. Don't you worry."

"And the skull with a bullet hole in it?" I eased the rope over the landing post, then leaned back, making no effort to get out of my comfortable seat. "You know stories, don't you?" I tried to look directly into the old man's eyes.

"Stories, yes, but they sometimes get mixed up. I've heard lots of things about this part of the swamp, but didn't always see it firsthand. One story I tell about somebody might be about some-body different altogether." He fanned his face. The water lapped gently against the boat.

"Tell me one," I said, grateful for the overhanging trees that cut off the hot rays.

"Where to start?"

"Ladies first," I said. "Alice."

Pasquin chuckled, pressed the straw hat atop his head and pulled it somewhat over his eyes. "Now, don't hold me to this 'cause it could have been some other woman."

I nodded and made a gesture with my hand that he should proceed.

"Now I think the family name was Calder. Alice Calder. She had about three sisters. Her momma died real young, and the poppa took in women off and on to help raise the girls. His idea, as was most poppa's back then, was to marry them all off and get on with his life. But something happened. He had gone off to war. Came back far as I know. Seems to me somebody told me he got captured over there." Pasquin stuck his fingers under his hat and scratched his head. He shrugged. "Anyhow, all his stuff got shipped back here. Now this I know because I remember hearing barge men talk about delivering a uniform, guns, and all that stuff."

"And the four daughters?" I urged Pasquin who had stopped to ponder something in the ancient recesses of his memory.

"Seems like the older three got married eventually. Alice, being the youngest, was still an old maid and everybody referred to her as just that. She got courted by this one and that one, but none of it took." Pasquin slapped at a buzzing mosquito.

"So when did she become Crazy Alice and start hanging out in the swamp?"

"Just eased into it, I guess. She didn't hang out in the swamp. Her daddy's house was up a ways on the bay and she lived there for a long time. Finally sold it to somebody in town. That fellow tore it down or let it rot. Not sure what's there now."

"And where did Alice go?"

Pasquin lifted both hands and shrugged. "Not sure. Rumor has it she bought this little fish hut way back yonder." He pointed into the forest. "It was on a corner of some land a man owned back there. Had lots of little cabins and stuff, along with a main house.

He went out fishing not too long ago, in the Gulf, and never came back. His family finally sold off the place."

"So Alice lived in the family home until she bought this little cabin, and that's probably where she resides today?"

"Could be, won't swear to it."

"And Jacob?"

Pasquin stared silently into space, then smiled. "You know I recall a story about Alice and Jacob being talked about as a number at one time." He laughed. "If it's true, old Jacob would have been toward the end of her hopes-for-a-husband career." He slapped his knee. "Old fool just has her come in and clean now. Wouldn't live with her nor anybody else."

"Then he's got the best of both worlds," I said. "No wife to support, especially a crazy one, but she'll still come in and clean for him." I frowned. "Southern males," I said under my breath.

"Ain't that something?" Pasquin seemed to be thinking deeply. He either didn't hear or ignored my comment on males.

"What's something?"

"Alice still goes around saying she's got her a man. Ain't never really had one, but she's still looking."

"What happened to her sisters?"

"May be all dead now. Moved away anyhow. Hadn't heard a thing about them in years."

"Wonder why Jacob never said anything about Alice being an old sweetheart that day we were with him," I said.

"Well," he stretched the word out two syllables. "It just might not be so."

Pasquin pulled the boat around where we could grab hold of the post and step onto the landing. It's rotting boards had to be negotiated carefully as rusty nails protruded and, in spots, gaps in the slats revealed the shallow, grass-filled water below.

I turned to help him, but he brushed me away and took hold of the post. His grunt was no louder than mine as he conquered the lift from the boat. I let him take the lead, and within three steps from the landing, we walked into the forest.

The lane from this side was clearer, though narrow and bordered by the encroaching trees and shrubs. We had to walk single file.

"Most people going out use this lane rather than go by way of Grandpa's Creek," said Pasquin. He removed his straw hat and batted at branches that got in his path. "Young man's trailer ain't too far from here."

We skirted sharp brambles and eased between close growing pine trunks until the area cleared and we stood a few yards from the dilapidated structure that served as a research center.

"Look there," said Pasquin as he pointed under the rusty fittings of the trailer.

"Sam Nettleson has a visitor," I said as I watched the sleek brown body of a snake disappear into the wild grass growing just below the rust. "He'd better be careful where he steps in those sandals."

We moved to the front, cautious about the snake that had just sought refuge beneath the trailer. Pasquin moved on around to the side, came back and rapped on the flimsy door.

"Doesn't seem to be to home," he said.

"Could be napping." I rapped harder and the door slipped open. "Mr. Nettleson?" I called twice, then pushed on the door. Standing on the top of the rickety steps, I peeked around through the opening. Humid odors that seemed a mix of spices and dirty water greeted me.

"Looks more like a big slumber party than a research lab," I said. I motioned for Pasquin to look inside at the sleeping bag on the floor. "Not much room here for anything."

"What's that stuff on the counter?" Pasquin shielded his eyes, trying for a better look at the wooden slat crates that sat on what was once the kitchen counter.

"Could be the containers for his samples," I said. "Only they look a bit deep for that." I backed down the steps and shrugged. "Well, who knows? I'm no scientist. Maybe we'll ask Nettleson to show us his so-called lab when he gets back."

We headed away from the trailer with its snake in the grass. The lane to Jacob's little cement abode took on the appearance of a disappearing passage in a kid's magic movie. The grasses and shrubs had decided to meet in the middle. Pasquin again used his hat to push it aside and make a way for us.

"Looks like somebody's making another way," he said when he stopped abruptly and pointed to his right.

I stretched my neck and focused my eyes on a narrow lane that had no bush interference and appeared to have tracks still in the damp earth. "How in the world did you know that was there?"

"Too much thinning out of the woods," he said and held some brambles out of the way.

We worked sideways into the forest until we stood on the used lane.

"Follows the other one parallel," he said and eyed the ground like a bloodhound. "Maybe Jacob done found a better way to get to Scrapper Creek."

"Or maybe Nettleson has," I said. Less than ten feet in front of us stood Sam Nettleson. He had a dolly stacked with two large crates like those in his trailer.

CHAPTER SEVEN

The surprise lasted seconds too long. I had the feeling Nettleson wanted to drop the dolly and run back into the forest. When he finally relaxed, he said, "Supplies came in."

Pasquin and I stared at the crates.

"More vials for samples?" I asked

He looked down at the unlabeled crates in front of him. The fresh, thin wood slats appeared recently nailed together. "Some of that, yeah." He looked at us for a while longer. "Uh, you know, we're not going to all be able to use this lane at one time."

Pasquin had said nothing until now. He moved backwards into the bushes and held the brambles back for me. I leaned into them with him. Nettleson lifted the dolly on its wheels and edged past us too quickly. The dolly tilted slightly. Pasquin put out a hand to balance the top crate. Grunting from the awkwardness, Nettleson sat the dolly back on its all-fours. After a moment, he lifted it again and headed down the lane. His sandals made prints over the ones going the opposite way.

"Now that's about the lightest test tubes I ever knew about," said Pasquin. He had moved back into the lane and watched Nettleson disappear into the trees on the way to his trailer. "Looked like green packing, too." He turned his attention back to his feet. "Wonder where this leads." He kicked up some dirt on the path.

"Shouldn't be hard to find out," I said and began walking down the trodden dirt. "Following dolly ruts and sandal prints doesn't take an old Indian."

"You mean an old Cajun!" Pasquin chuckled and followed me.

We retraced Nettleson's tracks until the path widened and ended suddenly on a sharp slant of a creek bank.

"Would you look at this!" said Pasquin as he fanned away a horse fly. "A creek I never knew about."

The bank had no grass. It appeared unnatural for this part of the forest. "It ends right here," I said and bent over to peer through the trees at the water lane, wide enough for at least one small motor boat.

"It's not natural," said Pasquin. He had stooped to rub some soil between his fingers. "Somebody cut this lane in here."

"University perhaps?" I said. "Maybe they did it to help with their researchers."

Pasquin looked at the watery lane then back at the bank. "Tie up over here." He pointed to a cement post sticking out of the sand at the bottom of the bank. "No ma'am, this ain't natural."

"Seems like they would have built a landing if it's to haul in supplies," I said.

"Don't make sense. Supplies could be hauled in from Scrapper Creek to that trailer better than from here." He stooped again and took up more earth between his fingers. He touched it as though the soil itself could speak to him and send a message, osmosis-like, through his flesh. "Nope, not natural anyway you look at it."

"Guess we'd better inform Amado."

Pasquin nodded and we headed back toward the main path, then trampled over swamp scrub to the overgrown path that led to Jacob's cement hovel. Pasquin led the way, quiet and forgetting to bat at sticky nettles that scraped along our waists. He stopped abruptly and peered between two tree trunks. Jacob's house stood cold and quiet in front of us.

"Ain't about, most likely," said Pasquin. He had stiffened and his forehead frowned under his hat.

"Is something wrong?" I whispered.

"Got a feeling," he said. "You stay here a minute."

Pasquin pushed between the trees and circled the cement block house, his old man body bending only at the neck. He disappeared around one side. I held my breath until he appeared around the other. He shrugged toward my position in the forest, then headed for the front door. He knocked several times but no one responded. He made a waving notion for me to come out of hiding.

"I guess I'll do it the old-fashioned way," he said and gave his loud "Whooooeee." That startled me and every critter in the surrounding area. Birds took flight from a nearby tree.

"No one," I said. "Do you think he's okay?"

Pasquin didn't answer for a moment, then said, "Out fishing or hunting. Something like that. Could have gone to town for staples." He looked about him into the forest. "No. Getting too close to dark. Let's go."

"It's not four yet," I said. "Lots of light for a while."

Pasquin ignored my comment. "You coming?" He headed back toward the lane.

We skirted around Nettleson's trailer on our way to the boat. His door was open and a cat sat on the steps, cleaning itself. A dead lizard lay on the top step, the cat's donation to his room and board.

Pasquin said nothing until we got back into his boat and were nearly out of Scrapper Creek.

"Okay, old man, tell me what's going on. You're too quiet, and it's not indigestion." I felt a chill off the water even though the air had to be ninety degrees.

"Got a feeling," he said. "Animals weren't right. Air seemed empty."

"You don't think Jacob was lying helpless in his house, do you?"

"Didn't see anybody through the windows. Maybe you ought to get that sheriff to check up on him when you tell him about the man-made creek."

"Can't you go with me and tell him yourself?"

"I got to do something. Check with some acquaintances of mine beyond the brackish water. You go on and call soon as I drop you off."

I stood on my landing and watched Pasquin back his boat into the river again and head for the brackish water. He would pull into someone's landing and walk through the swamp to whomever he wanted to visit. His rigid old body sat at the throttle and guided the boat through the cypress trees until he hit open water. His hat in one hand, his egret white hair blowing straight back in the breeze, he disappeared around a bend of low hanging oaks.

"You want me to check on a constructed creek in the woods, and an old hermit who lives back there?" Tony Amado was being Tony Amado. He questioned my every request, a slight sneer in his voice that wanted to say, "Woman, what the hell are you talking about?"

"I'm telling you about it, Tony. You got a skull with a bullet hole and a missing kid's body. Now I'm telling you about a scraped-out water way, an old swamp man that may or may not be in jeopardy, plus a university kid hauling supplies along a new forest lane." I took a deep breath. "If you don't want to check it out, then don't." I waited. Amado always took the bait when I tossed the line in his direction.

"You get over to your university and look up that Nettleson researcher. See if his department really is sponsoring such a thing. I'll get to the other stuff when I can." I knew he meant right now.

Tony, in spite of his argumentative nature, would not dispute the intuition of an old swamp man like Pasquin.

I sat on my landing. The only thing between the river's edge and my front porch was the narrow dirt lane just big enough for one car. My own blue '84 Honda station wagon rested under the carport. It had seen me through changes in scuba tanks and gear over the years as well as daily treks into Tallahassee to teach college linguistic classes. I had to deal with my own restlessness, get around the leaden feeling of drudgery each time the fall semester began. It was the endless round of lectures, giving tests, and assigning papers.

Not to mention grading them. Lately, the Internet had invaded everything and student cheating ran amok. I could spend hours checking out sources where some sophomore decided to forgo a dialect project based on oyster fishermen in Apalachicola and copy data right off his computer. When the end of the term arrived, I felt the black cloud move away. My swamp house beckoned, along with the cool spring waters. I was dwelling on all this, refusing to make the trip to campus to question the sciences about their water research projects until I built up the energy, when a motor boat sped past me. A nasty whine of its engine penetrated the woods. Two girls with baseball caps and sunglasses sat in the front seats, one steering.

"Slow down!" I yelled into their wake, but they wouldn't have heard me. I watched as they raced around a bend and disappeared.

My reverie lost, I sighed and headed for the Honda. It would take me twenty minutes to bump over the rutted road, then take two paved roads to the streets of Tallahassee.

I parked outside the new brick building that housed biological sciences. It was not a place I had knowledge of, but seemed the

right place to begin. My own linguistics building was an older, gothic
-style structure across campus.

The few students on campus strolled about, sweating in shorts
and tees, stopping only for a little fondling in the grass before the
next class began. It looked like a slow summer session. The building itself seemed deserted until I walked down an echoing hallway
and found an office. Inside, one student secretary clicked away on a
computer.

"Where do I find someone who can tell me about research
projects?" I leaned over a vacant desk in her direction, but the student didn't look away from her monitor.

"What kind?" She said into the glare.

"River water." I moved to her side.

She didn't move her eyes away from her work, and her fingers
continued to click. "Don't know anything about that."

"Who would?" I eyed her tank top and low-cut pants. She was
an older version of Roxanna.

"We do animal stuff here. Try second floor."

"Office number?"

She finally looked at me and shrugged. "Second floor."

Would the entire world become like this, I wondered. People
who stuck to their machines and brushed off fellow humans with a
shrug? I sighed and headed upstairs.

ECOLOGICAL SCIENCES spelled itself across a sign stuck
on an office door at the end of one hallway. I pushed it open. The
same desertion was apparent here. One student, a male with a shaved
head and bare feet sat at a desk. He leaned back in his swivel chair,
his feet—with dirty toes—stuck on top of the desk. He sucked on
a straw from a paper cup and read a magazine.

"Yeah?" He said, again without looking up.

"What's with the generation of no eye contact?" I wanted to

grab his magazine and slap his dirty feet out of sight.

"Huh?" He finally looked up at me.

"I need to get some information about students doing water research." I stood directly over him, both hands on my hips.

"Can't just give out stuff like that. Who are you?"

"Professor Luanne Fogarty, Linguistics Department," I said and smiled at him.

"What do you need to know?" He slapped the magazine on the desk.

I leaned over and took it. "Guns? You are in the Ecology Department and you like guns?" I tossed it back onto the desk.

He shrugged and removed his feet.

"That's better," I said.

"What do you want?" His face still had that adolescent look of fright and defiance at the same time.

"Who among the students here is doing research on the Palmetto River water?"

He stared at me a while then shrugged again. "Don't know."

"Can you find out? Please."

He looked around him at empty desks and stretched his neck toward a closed office in the back of the room. "Doubt it. Nobody is here this time of the year. I just stay around to take messages and stuff like that."

"And stuff like that? Well, when will someone who knows things get your messages?" I tapped a finger on his computer monitor.

"Don't know. Depends if anyone checks in or not. It's just a bad time of year." He watched my finger move across the computer.

"Try looking it up," I said and pointed to the keyboard.

"I'm not sure I—"

"Okay, move aside and let me try."

"No! I'll do it." He hit some keys. "But you got to know I only have a list of graduate students and their projects. Can't get you any data that might be secret." He moved his eyes across the booted up monitor.

"Not looking for secrets." I bent over his shoulder and helped him look.

A list of names came up with projects listed beside them.

"Ph.D. candidates?"

"Could be," he said. "Graduate students anyway."

He scrolled down the list. "No Nettleson, and no Palmetto River," I said. "Can you print this out for me?"

"No!" His face paled. "I wouldn't dare do that."

"Then could you get me a drink of water?" I nodded toward the cooler near the office door.

The student looked at the monitor then at me and finally got up and went to the cooler. I hit the print command. On the way out the door, I told him to drink the water himself and asked what his specialty was in the department.

"Earth-borne viruses," he said.

I turned around and stared at his dirty toes. "Oh," I said and left with the list.

I traveled south again, the list on the seat beside me. I thought about the dirty-footed graduate student and Roxanna's butt tattoo and wondered what the next generation would look like when these two reproduced.

Back at my porch, I heard a motor boat go speeding back the other way. It had the same sound as the one the girls were in when they tore past me.

Plato greeted me at the door, his entire back body wagging furiously.

"You need food, right?"

Inside, I scooped out the ripe-smelling dog food and left him to slurp it up in the kitchen.

"Tony," I spoke into the phone to voice mail, "so far nothing on Nettleson from the college. I've got a list of graduate students and their current projects. E-mail addresses are here, too, so I think I'll just ask around. It's going to take an officer with a badge to get much out of the department."

Inside the cool of my living room, I leaned back in the recliner and opened the list. Almost every person there was doing some kind of research based on water. Our area, long known to be about as wet as any place can get, had suffered a long, nasty drought lately. Much of the research was in the direction of bacteria in sinkholes and the lowering of the water tables. Only one had anything to do with water quality. I circled his name.

CHAPTER EIGHT

"Come on over to the Lake Jackson facility, and I'll be happy to talk to you about whatever you want to know." The e-mail message was signed Georgie. That was the Georgie Emment from the list. I had asked him a vague question about water quality studies.

Lake Jackson was a string of water pockets on both sides of Highway 27 west of town. Easily seen from a plane, it signaled the approach to the airport. Most years, it sat full and gave a place to fish and frolic for most who lived along its sides. Recently, however, it had drained itself twice down a sinkhole that unplugged during a drought. Turtles, fish, and debris left by boaters all got sucked down a hole that would find a water lane deep within the earth. Behind, it left a sticky bacteria growing on the sides of the hole.

I parked on the side of the highway and walked through the marsh grass to a tent where two men sat with lap computers, papers, and vials of gooey white stuff that looked a lot like snot.

"Georgie?"

An odd-shaped man with wispy balding hair looked up and grinned. He squinted through thick glasses. Hitting a key, he closed the lap computer and said, "Georgie Porgie with no pudding pie. You got me anyway you want me."

"I'm Luanne Fogarty," I said and put out my hand.

"Oh, the e-mail lady. God! You look nothing like the vision I had in my head." He brushed his hand on a tee shirt that read *Bio*

70

Territorialist, then shook mine.

"Sorry."

"Oh, no! Don't apologize. I thought you'd be some dumpy thing in sweats with stringy hair.

The other student chuckled. "He's not too tactful, ma'am."

"Neither am I." I turned back to Georgie. "Have you any knowledge of a student colleague named Sam Nettleson?"

The two men gazed at each other, both with silly grins on their faces. Georgie turned his face up to mine, getting an eye full of sun rays. He winced and looked away.

"Why do you want to know?"

"Just helping out the sheriff on a murder case," I said. I had an adjunct diver card with the sheriff's department emblem on it. I whipped it out.

"Oooooo," both men said as they gazed at the badge.

"Well, now," said Georgie, "I remember a Nettleson from some classes I took a while back. Don't think he's doing water research, but I could be mistaken. Sometimes these projects get approved at the last minute. And then sometimes grant money comes in late."

"Yeah, Sam Nettleson," said the other student.

Georgie gazed at his friend then began to nod. "Right. I guess we kind of see specimens clearer than we see our fellow humans."

"Any way you can find out if he's doing a study?"

Both men shrugged. "Maybe."

"I see." I stood silently until Georgie pulled up one of the snot filled vials and waved it in front of me.

"Now this is real!" He laughed. "Ask me about cave bacteria, and I can identify several types."

"Yes, I know," I said. "I once had to go down into a sinkhole and I got that stuff all over me."

The men stared at each other.

"Will I get a devastating disease?"

"If you don't already have one, I guess not." Georgie's expression changed to admiring blinks of his weak eyes. "Say," he looked at his fellow researcher and moved off the chair. "You want to see where the stuff came from?"

"I know where it came from, but, yeah, show me." I followed the man who seemed to be two circles cinched at the waist. He wore oversized military pants with pockets down each leg.

We stood overlooking the main sinkhole. Research cavers were inside, their gear attached to the sides and reinforced by stakes farther from the area.

Georgie pointed downward. "I really didn't want to show you this. I wanted to talk to you away from…" He nodded toward his research mate. "We're stuck out here doing this stuff, and frankly I'm bored silly. You need help on a murder case?" He waited for me to nod. "I can help you, I'm sure. Here's my card. You already have my e-mail. I'll do some snooping in the department. Even ask around the state ecological departments and see if this Nettleson is with them." He grinned and squinted at me. I was reminded of the old Mr. McGoo cartoons I had seen as a child.

"Thanks," I said. "How familiar are you with the waterways in the county?"

He shrugged. "I got more maps than Magellan. If I don't know them, I can find them. Uh, but one thing." He hung his head like a bad child. "I can't swim."

"I can," I said and waved as I turned to go to the car. "I'll be in touch." I passed him a card where he could reach me.

"Our secret," he said and grinned into the sun. I wondered if he could see me more than a few yards away.

On the way back, I phoned Tony and told him I had someone working on the Nettleson connection.

"I'm going to use the canoe on Grandpa's Creek and see if I can find a water lane," I said.

"Stay away from there, Luanne. Unless you've got Vernon with you."

"You're breaking up," I said and turned off the phone. If I heeded Tony's every order, I'd be sitting in my living room and dreaming up scenarios of what could happen.

I turned into my carport and stopped short of pulling the car all the way underneath it. My trusty canoe rested against the wall. Attaching it to the ancient gear on top of the Honda wasn't easy, and I often had this feeling I'd look into the rearview mirror one day and see it sliding down the highway pavement. But, I finally secured it. Tossing in a diving mask, some high boots, and my pistol, I headed for Grandpa's Creek off the brackish water area of Palmetto River.

A few fishermen leaned against their truck bumpers, sipping beer, and waiting for the tide so they could put their outboards in and see what the afternoon might bring. They smiled at me as I shoved the canoe into the water. I didn't need to wait for the tide.

Rowing through thick grass and shallow water slowed me down, but when I reached the end of Grandpa's Creek, I realized that there were no off lanes that might take me elsewhere. I shoved the canoe onto the marsh grass area and lay the oars under the seat. Pulling on my high boots and tucking the pistol into my waistband, I stepped into the thick swamp. I wanted to find a pond or some kind of water space that would allow someone from a road to put in a boat and move down that man-made lane.

The going was rough. I stepped into high scrub in several places, holding my breath that I wouldn't have to whip out the pistol and shoot a rattlesnake. Once, a streamlined deer darted in front of me and leapt over the scrub until it disappeared into the trees. I must have walked in a circle of maybe two miles, but nothing looked like water. At one point, I came into a clearing, a place where someone had removed the scrub and placed some stones in a circle. The middle, solid dirt, had been raked. I stood on the stones and walked around the circle. In my mind, I could see Satanic teens using this for some foolhardy idea of religious rites. When I leaned against a tree, something fell and made me reach for the gun. It was a rake. It had been leaning against the tree. As I scoured the swamp around the area for other evidence of human invention, I heard a gasp behind me. Pulling out the pistol, I turned and saw nothing but trees. It was a Mexican standoff. Neither of us moved. I finally lowered my hand with the pistol and turned away from the clearing. Rapid breaking of underbrush disturbed the silence, and I turned just in time to see sandals and a muu-muu flashing into the trees.

"She's wandering the swamp, Tony," I said as I sat on the bank where my canoe was supposed to be waiting for me. "She did something to my transportation. You need to send Vernon." I hated this. I was admitting into my cell phone that I was stranded at the end of Grandpa's Creek, on a journey Tony had told me not to take.

"Up the creek without a paddle," Tony had said. He may have chuckled at his own joke, but since I'd never heard a chuckle out of him before, I didn't know what he was doing. "I'll see what I can spare. Just sit there and don't go wandering into the woods."

"Are you going to look into Crazy Alice's jaunts?"

"No law against that unless she's trespassing on private land, and I don't think that's the case."

I sat on the wet ground until my back hurt. When I lay on the same ground, I felt better until I came face to face with a string of fire ants. I sat up and shuffled away from their parade. Tony was taking his time. I leaned over and watched the tide rise into the creek. Eel grass undulated just below the surface, giving the water lane an appearance of being alive. I thought I'd find my canoe below that surface, but there was no sign of it. Someone must have stolen it by paddling it right out of the creek.

"Yo! Luanne!" It was Loman, steering a sheriff's department power boat through the narrow lane and waving at me at the same time. He jerked hard to his right, causing a wake to splash on shore.

"I don't need a bath, Loman. Jeez!" I swiped at the creek water that landed in muddy spots below my knees.

"Hey, we tried to get your old friend to come after you, but we couldn't raise him." Loman held the wheel and leaned over to give me a hand. The boat lurched.

"Just turn the boat off, okay," I said and stood back until he maneuvered it next to the bank again. He switched it off and sat down. "Good, now just sit there and I'll use you as a balance."

I stepped in, one hand resting on Loman's shoulder. He grabbed the side of the boat when it rocked with my weight.

"Pasquin?" I said as I sat in the passenger seat.

"Yeah, him. Tried calling him at his house, Mama's Table, and a couple of other places. Nobody's seen him."

"Tony ordered you to come?" I told myself that Pasquin had mentioned seeing someone he knew and that he often headed off down river lanes.

"Vernon was busy," Loman said and looked around as though asking himself how the hell to back out of here.

"Wait!" I said. "It's not dark yet. Let's take a little walk."

"Luanne." Loman drawled it out, but he was no match for a woman. He let me hold the boat while he climbed out.

"Take the key to this thing. I wouldn't want the same thief to run off with a sheriff's boat."

Loman followed me as best he could, but for a good old boy who should have been taught to hunt, he was awkward in the woods. Every branch, bramble and mud hole waited for him. He batted mosquitoes and sweated buckets.

"What do you want to go looking for that old man for?" He finally said.

"Because Jacob wasn't in his house when I looked with Pasquin. I want to see if he returned."

"No crime if he hasn't," said Loman. He turned his ankle and fell into the bushes. Wet, moldy leaves clung to his pants leg.

"Not necessarily," I said. "It's just around here."

We came into the clearing in front of the cement block house that said PARADISE over the door. Silence prevailed.

I knocked on the door, then skirted around to all the windows, knocking and calling Jacob's name. Loman followed me like an over-sized puppy.

"Ain't nobody here," he said.

"Let's see." I walked straight to the front door and turned the handle. It opened.

"Luanne! We'll need a search warrant."

"Even if we suspect he's in danger?"

Loman shrugged and followed me inside.

The sparse furniture sat neatly, without dust, as before. I walked into the kitchen, then down the hall and stood in the tiny bedroom and bath. The bed was made, the bathroom cleaned. It was tidier than any place I knew, including my own.

"Alice must have been here," I said.

"Alice?"

"Jacob says she cleaned for him. Looks like this was just done."

"No sign of the old guy." Loman went to the high kitchen window, stood on his toes to look out, then lost his balance and fell against the counter.

"Ever take ballet?" I left the room before he could answer.

We rode silently down the creek lane, back to Palmetto River. Loman let me steer until we reached the roped off area. He stopped picking briars off his pants and took over, not wanting his male pals to see that he had given command of a sheriff's boat over to a woman who was a part-time employee.

"Any word from Pasquin?" I asked as Tony met us at the dock.

"None." He let a uniformed deputy help me out of the boat. No one helped Loman who swayed and for a moment looked as though he'd go over the side. "And nobody around this part of the river has seen him today."

"I'll go by his house. Anybody check my house?" Pasquin often sat on my front porch until I came home. Many times I had found him sound asleep there, in the dark in a rocking chair.

"Vernon went by there. No Pasquin."

I told Tony of the journey back to Jacob's house and finding no one around. Nodding and shrugging was about all the response I would get for now.

"You think the two old men are together?"

"No," I said. "Pasquin instinctively knew he was not at home, and I think he went to find out something."

"Where?"

I stood there, suddenly stunned. Jacob had disappeared. Why not Pasquin, too? Two old swamp men, lost.

CHAPTER NINE

"You know how to get into his house?" Vernon followed me down the lane that lead from my house to Pasquin's. It had been a familiar path for both of us, one that led to good friends. And my good friend had let me know he was going to look into something.

"An eighty-plus old man won't stay away from his comfortable bed for long," I had told myself when I couldn't rouse Pasquin by phone. "I know where he hides a key," I said aloud to Vernon.

We dodged thorny vines that grew across the path like railroad guards. Tossing one back, it reflexed quickly and hit me across the arm. Tiny blood spots appeared, and I rubbed at them with a tissue.

Pasquin's house, one he had built himself many years ago, stood in a clearing like a haven in a storm of jungle flora and fauna. It was a one-story version of my place, wood-framed, fading white paint, a screened porch in front. He had added a storage shed in the back to house his garden tools. Beyond that lay another clearing where he grew beans, peas, and pumpkins or whatever he fancied during the season. "Peppers don't do good in this soil," I'd heard him say many times. "Ol' Cajun will just have to buy his peppers."

Vernon motioned me to stay back a moment. He skirted the house, looking into windows that were heavily draped. He disappeared to one side. I stood in uneasy silence until he reappeared from behind the shed.

"Nothing," he said. "Can't see inside for these drapes." Pasquin prided himself on the thickest, darkest drapes he could buy. "Keeps the heat out," he'd say.

I walked with Vernon onto the front porch. "Screen is unlatched. He's not here," I said, knowing he could be in there but unable to reach the door. I knocked that from my brain. Life without Pasquin just down the swamp path was not imaginable.

Vernon rapped on the door. When no one came, I headed for the front steps. They rose off the swamp floor, three cement slabs supported by rods anchored in the ground. I leaned under the top step and ran my hand over the underbelly of rough cement. I hit a chiseled out groove, just large enough for a house key.

"Clever place," said Vernon. "Just better look for snakes before you go crawling into that space."

"I think that's why he rigged the notch. Nobody is going to grope around there by choice." I handed Vernon the key.

"Let me go in first," he said, and pulled his pistol. I stood to one side. After what seemed an eternity, he yelled from the back room, "nobody here!"

Inside the living room, the locked up heat hit me like a wet electric blanket. Dark green curtains blocked out all light, and the rickety window air-conditioner had not done its job at all that day.

I searched with Vernon in the back bedroom, the closets and bathroom used by this ancient swamp hermit. Feeling as low as an invading termite, I searched his Sunday suit that he never wore, and fingered through drawers full of carelessly folded shorts and socks.

"Where does the man do his laundry?" asked Vernon as he sifted through a clothes hamper.

"Washer and drier in the shed," I said. "He put them in one year when the old swamp lady who did it for him died." I lifted the box Pasquin kept under his bed. His stash of silver dollars looked untouched.

"Shouldn't he have those in a bank?"

"He does have the bulk of them in a safety deposit box. These he keeps around for rainy days. I guess he feels if they are stolen, he can live without them." I shut the top. "Not even a lock."

Back in the living room, we skirted the overstuffed chairs, sofas and coffee tables until we found a clearing near a tiny television that sat next to the fireplace.

"The man needs a garage sale," said Vernon as he stubbed his toe on one of the two rockers inside the house.

"He buys new stuff but refuses to get rid of the old," I said, remembering many nights when Pasquin would gather his fellow swampers here for drinks and boiled peanuts. Sometimes they'd sing country songs way into the night, and if the wind blew right, I could hear them on my own front porch. The agitation began in the pit of my stomach and moved upward until my eyes teared up. To shove off the feeling, I headed for the kitchen.

"His pills," I said. "He wouldn't leave them if he were staying overnight somewhere."

I looked through the wicker basket Pasquin kept on the tiny dining table at one end of the room. "Nothing but over the counter stuff here."

"What does he take?"

"I think some blood pressure stuff, but there are none here."

"Good sign." Vernon pulled me close. "Luanne, he's gone to check something like he said, and is staying with a swamp buddy."

I let it go then, all the built up feelings of abandonment or loss or whatever they were, and sobbed into Vernon's chest.

Later, when we were walking back to my place, I turned to him. "If we find him and he's okay, just don't tell him I broke into baby wails."

Approaching my porch, I hoped to see Pasquin where he often was when I returned home, rocking and fanning himself with his hat. Instead, I saw Harry MacAllister resting on the middle step.

He took a look at Vernon, then glanced at me. "It's the day we agreed to..." He looked at Vernon again.

The sweat poured off me, and I wanted to scream into the forest. Instead, I turned to Vernon. "Harry needs help in going down again, especially into caves. He's asked me to help." I looked him straight in the eyes. "Do you think it's possible he can overcome his fear?"

Vernon, my anchor on sanity at times like these, came through again. "It's possible. Come on. All three of us will dive."

Harry lowered his head then looked back up at me with the guilt of a dog who ate the family dinner. I smiled back at him.

Suited and tanked, we hit the water off my landing. The water felt icy for a while, shocking me into reality. We dived in the river, going deeper and deeper until Harry motioned to his leg. Back at the landing, he said, "It gets to hurting when I get deep, like the water is squeezing the vessels."

"Just move it around some," said Vernon. "Most likely it's psychological."

We dove twice more and each time Harry came up with the same excuse. Back on the landing, we removed the tanks and sat in the warm sun.

"Unless you stay down there, the pain won't quit," I said. "If the doctors say there is no reason for this, then it's in your head, not in the water, or the cave."

Harry nodded without speaking. His full head of wavy hair dried in the sun. I once admired that hair, and those lean muscles that dove into caves dark as pitch. Now, he was a man whose jaw ground around words he couldn't speak because of the terror that had set in from the underwater bomb.

Vernon was watching me when I turned toward him. His own bald pate glistened with water droplets and would soon blister in the sun unless he donned his cap. He winked at me. I held his hand. Not many lovers would allow an ex-lover to intrude like this. Later, he said it was a diving thing. That if something like that had happened to him, he would hope Harry and other divers would help him.

"Well, I'll always help you," I whispered as we drifted into sleep long after Harry had packed his gear and left. Vernon hugged me and grunted before turning over, his breathing heavy with deep slumber.

Morning came too early and with a heavy depression. I had visions of Pasquin on the river, stranded somewhere and unable to get his boat started. "But he'd know how to signal some swamp hermits," I said as I flipped on the coffee maker. I had tried calling his house twice, but still no answer. Vernon greeted me with a sheepish smile.

"All that swimming put me in a deep sleep," he said. "I might be late." He sipped coffee and downed cereal while wrapped in a towel.

"Vernon, I'm going to borrow a boat and look for Pasquin," I said, suddenly realizing my need for a motor boat had always been fulfilled by Pasquin.

"Not by yourself."

"Can you get off?"

"You kidding? Tony's got work for me this morning."

"Then who?"

"I'll ask if there's an off duty deputy who can ride with you."

The phone rang before I could wave off his suggestion. "It's Tony. How late are you?"

Vernon spoke to Tony at length, something about the Hanover family. I took my coffee to the front porch and sat in the morning mist. Already the humidity enclosed the small space, wrapping me in steam bath heat. The river seemed busy with fishermen moving about in their boats. Their slow putt-putts pulled into coves where bass or cat fish were biting. Suddenly in the midst of the calm, the power boat flew by. I couldn't see it from the porch, but I knew the sound. Fisherman yelled curses at the pilot. No one should be riding like that on this segment of the river.

"We're to meet Tony at the Hanover place. He's already on his way. Seems the man wants the cops out of his son's search and has hired his own detective diver." Vernon pulled a white undershirt over his head.

"Who's patrolling the river for speed boats right now?" I followed Vernon into the house.

"Not sure," he shrugged.

We drove through one swamp, onto the highway, then back into another part of the forest until we arrived at the river entry to Grandpa's Creek. Loman waited with a sheriff's pilot. We'd take the boat to the landing off Hanover's place to meet Tony.

The going was excruciatingly slow. It was the area of manatee warning signs and boats could travel only at the lowest speeds. A boat traveling at the maddening pace Tommy Hanover ran his would certainly hit one of the endangered animals.

"You think that kid deliberately hit the manatee?" I asked as Loman sat in his seat but leaned sideways to hold onto the side.

"Maybe. I don't put a thing past these kids." He jumped as the boat hit a small wake. "Got too much money and not enough brains."

Hanover's landing was at the bottom of a newly built deck. The wood hadn't grayed yet. On it, sat a grill and a blue-and-white deck set. We tied up and walked up the bank to the front of the house. Its natural wood rose into the spreading oaks to two stories. "Must be over 2,000 square feet," I said.

"Nice way to vacation. Wonder what the house in town looks like." Loman stumbled on the incline and Vernon helped him the rest of the way.

Tony paced at his car. "Look, the man is angry. He thinks we can't find his son, so he's going to tackle it himself. You need to convince him you can find the body, only say *the boy*, not *the body*." We followed him to the front door.

The woman who answered could have been an older sister of one of Tommy's girlfriends. She wore shorts with a tank top and pulled her hair into a pony tail atop her head.

"Pamela Hanover," she said and put out her hand. A large diamond ring was her only formal wear.

"You're Tommy's mother?" Vernon asked.

"Stepmother," she said with a half smile. "He and I only see each other on vacations and stuff. He usually stays with his mom in town."

"And his mom, isn't she worried?" I moved into the large room. It had a shotgun effect with the front room moving right to the back and opening onto the deck. A pungent odor drifted around on the air conditioning, something like incense mixed with pond water, a little like the odor of Nettleson's tacky trailer.

"Suppose so," Pamela shrugged. "She wouldn't tell me, of course." She flashed a wicked smile, like the other woman who ate up the first wife. "My husband has been in touch with her, of course."

"So has the sheriff's office," said Tony. "Could we see your husband?"

"He's not here. Went into town on business. But," she sighed and headed for the source of the incense odors. She pulled out another stick and held it against a match until it glowed. When she stuck it into the brass holder, she continued, "he wouldn't see you anyhow. He's got somebody else to try and find Tommy, a Mr. Chalker who dives for a salvage company."

"Look, ma'am," said Tony, he jaw working in agitation, "your husband has no choice. This is a police case and he has to talk to us."

Pamela threw up both hands and coyly peeked at Tony. "I'm just telling you what he said to me."

Vernon and Tony sat in two red chairs across from Pamela. Loman stood near the door, raising and lowering himself on his toes like a mechanical toy. At times he seemed to be attempting to peek into a small trash can sitting next to a writing desk. I moved to the glass doors that opened to the deck.

A round table stood near the door. It had been fashioned to look like a piece of a Roman column. On the marble top, lay some photos of the missing son. I sifted through them, pulling up one of Tommy and the two girls leaning on the deck railing. They were in bathing suits and deliberately pressing close together. With one hand, they raised beer bottles in a kind of toast to the good life and with the other, held cigarettes between their index fingers and thumbs, an obvious declaration of smoking pot. The youthful, ripe figures each sported a ring in a pierced belly button. This was the reason for the closeness. They wanted to show off the faddish mutilation of their young bodies. There were no photos of their backsides, but I wondered if maybe Tommy didn't also have a flower on his butt.

"Tell your husband that he can hire whomever he wants, but that person must stay out of our way. This is a sheriff's case." Tony faced the pert Pamela who shifted her tank top when she rose from the sofa. "And tell him to call me." He handed over his card, something her husband would surely already have.

"Sure you don't want to have some iced tea?" Pamela seemed oblivious to Tony's sternness. It was a ploy she must have often pulled when her husband voiced anger.

"Bimbo of the swamp," I said as we headed again for the boat.

"Plaything," said Vernon, a wide grin lighting up his face. "He bought his kid a power boat and himself a baby doll."

"And what's with the incense?" I asked.

"Covers up the pot, I imagine," said Loman. "Trash can was full of roll-your-own butts."

After a silent pause, Vernon said, "Idle rich."

We sat in the patrol boat and waited for the deputy to untie and pull into open water.

"Let's head down a few lanes," I said.

The pilot looked at Loman for an okay.

"Why not," he said. "Tony wants you to find the boy."

Vernon squeezed my hand and winked. "I don't think it's a young boy she's looking for right now."

CHAPTER TEN

The river is not kind. It doesn't cough up the dead, and it doesn't lead you to the living. At least that was my take on it. Pasquin would have said otherwise. He had become the river in many ways and knew how to read its map. We were in a lane near where I thought he might head. If his preoccupation with something secret bothered me yesterday, it scared me silly now.

"He hasn't ever done this before," I stood and searched the shore with my eyes. The trees were too thick. A black bear could have been hiding in one of the heavy oaks and I wouldn't know it.

"Sure he has. You used to say he goes off all the time," Vernon said and helped me look.

"No, not alone, or not telling me where he was headed. He'll go off with his swamp buddies sometimes, or head up to Mama's Table by himself, but this." I closed my eyes, trying not to imagine finding Old Man Pasquin drowned near some cypress roots.

"Who's that?" Vernon pointed into the water where a scuba tank cleared the surface. When the diver's face came out of the water, he lifted his mask and waved at us. Dragging himself to shore, he pulled off the tank and dropped to the ground. All of him collapsed except the little pot belly held in place by the wet suit.

"That's Hanover's diver, Mr. Chalker," said the deputy. "He's some old veteran that used to work for a salvage company down in the Keys. He kind of swims along the river and the creeks, searching the bottom like a catfish." He snickered as he turned the boat away. "Couldn't be going too deep. He's diving alone."

"What's down this way?" asked the deputy as he steered the boat slowly through heavy hydrilla growth. "Don't see any landings."

It wasn't a lane I knew. It was too close to the brackish water that led into the Gulf, too far from my corner of the forest.

"Let's go to the end if we can, see what's back here." I nodded to the pilot.

"Okay, but it's going to be slow in places. They haven't cleared this lane of hydrilla grass for some time, maybe never."

I shut my eyes for a moment, silently cursing the person who dumped aquarium grass into the springs and ruined them, probably forever.

The pilot yelled, "Hey! Canoe on shore."

Vernon stood in the boat, holding it steady by grasping the overhanging limbs of a tree. A canoe lay on its side on the bank, almost as if someone had rowed it quickly to the spot, then jumped out and abandoned it.

"It's mine!" I recognized the scratches from the sides of my old Honda. It scraped the canoe every time I shoved it into the rack.

"Whoever took it rowed quite a distance from Grandpa's Creek." Vernon stepped into the water, then turned and helped me out. We waded through water hyacinth to shore.

"It's damaged," said Vernon as he turned the canoe upright. "Someone has deliberately rammed a hole in this side."

"And with this, it seems." I picked up one of the oars. The end was broken from the impact, and it fit the hole.

"Let's walk a ways into the woods," said Vernon and motioned for the deputy to hold the patrol boat in place.

"Could be a path along here," I said as I shoved into the undergrowth. "Looks like some broken limbs and trampled mud."

The swamp here took on a primeval quality, an even more primitive area than the other fecund areas where one had to watch for the rattler or gator basking in the sun. There was almost no light coming through the thick tree limbs, and palmetto bushes grew in spiky clusters. They were preferred hiding places for snakes, and the ones here had not been disturbed for years. Whole colonies of wiggly things could be living beneath the bright green spires.

"This way," said Vernon. He had followed some muddy footprints in a gap between two large oak trunks. "The footprints look like someone was barefoot."

"Not too wise to walk in here without shoes," I said. I had visions of the old hookworm panic when I was in elementary schools. They showed us drawings of a barefoot kid stepping on soil and as he raised his foot, a hookworm grabbed hold and, evidently, entered his body to do terrible things to his guts. I shuddered.

"I hear water," I said as we stepped into a sandy black soil.

"There," said Vernon. "A natural spring bubbling up."

It was something out of an Irish myth. Water flowed up between two clumps of earth, popping bubbles and gurgling, then traveling into a shallow stream that led further into the forest.

"Could be a larger water path back here." Vernon stepped beside the stream, following it through the brush. "Yep. Just what I said." He stood aside and waved his hand to a creek. The stream of water led into it, the gush visible in the clarity.

"Not wide enough for a boat, but it looks deep."

"Might be a spot to dive and explore," he said.

I leaned over the bank. There was no hydrilla growing here. In spots, the water was shallow enough to see white bottom where a few strands of eel grass grew. But for most of the area, the depth kept the water black and its contents unknown.

"Has to be caves or springs down there," I said. "Something is feeding this besides the stream."

We stood in silence for a moment. The dark water gave out slight gurgling sounds every few seconds. Around us, the forest was nearly as dark as the water and grew darker. In the distance, thunder sounded its warning and lightning flashed.

"We'd better get back before the storm starts." Vernon pulled out a pocket knife. "I'm cutting some grooves so we'll find this place when we return."

By the time he had made the notches in trees along the trail, the wind had begun to blow and thunder edged closer. When we crawled back into the patrol boat, my damaged canoe tied onto the back, lightning streaked across the sky.

"Gonna get wet!" yelled the deputy as he turned the boat into the hydrilla grass. "Can't get you out of here fast."

He steered around the grass at what seemed a snail's pace. When he found open river, he revved the engine and we held on. Lightning flashed behind us as though chasing us off the river, away from its secrets.

"Get into the car," said Vernon. We jumped off the boat as soon as the deputy pulled it up to the landing at the police site near the bridge.

We had been soaked to the skin, and the excess water dripped onto the upholstery of the patrol car. Vernon pulled a towel from the rear seat and ran it across his face and head, then passed it to me. He radioed in to tell Tony of our find.

"I'm on my way there," said Tony. "Tell Luanne some guy named Georgie Emment has been calling for her."

"Emment?" I brushed the towel across my face and rubbed my arms. The sudden gush of air conditioning sent chills from my toes to my shoulders.

I pulled the cell phone from my bag and dialed the number Tony had given. The voice that went with the stuffed sausage body answered, nearly gushing with excitement.

"I found out stuff," he said. "And I might be able to show you something."

The storm wasn't over when I pulled the Honda into my muddy dirt drive on the edge of the Palmetto River. I shivered from the soaking and cool air. My hair rested against my head, refusing to dry. I probably looked as silly as Georgie Emment who stood on my front porch.

"Hope you don't mind," he said. "But this porch looked more inviting than the front seat of my van." He waved his hand toward a rusted white van that appeared to be packed with all sorts of boxes. "I kind of carry my lab around with me."

"You found the place fairly easily, I see." I stepped out and pulled my shirt away from my skin. I had given Georgie directions to meet me at my place, taking the chance that he'd be an up-and-up graduate student and not the village serial killer.

Georgie held the door for me. Today, his belt pulled in the blubber of a stomach and oversized hips with room to spare. The military pockets drooped down his legs, stretched from holding the instruments of a field scientist.

"I know this area," he grinned. "Been doing experiments all over these swamps."

"Look, I have to get out of these clothes. Wait downstairs for me. There's tea in the fridge, if you like." I trudged up the stairs, leaving Georgie grinning up after me. As I glanced at him from the top, I imagined him in all white; a giant marshmallow man image popped into my head.

In the middle of the shower, when I was soaped up and drenching myself clean, I wondered if Georgie might be some kind of nerdy killer, just standing outside my door, ready to pounce with a knife through the shower curtain. But when I shut off the water, I saw no shadow waiting to pull a Psycho on me. I heard, instead, whistling down stairs. "Okay," I whispered to myself, "the guy is The Whistler."

The serial killer who resembled two beach balls stacked on top of each other had raided the kitchen and come up with sustenance. A pot of coffee sat on the dining table, alongside a plate of strange looking toast.

"My own invention," he said. "Well, maybe my mom's, but I carry on the tradition."

He shoved the plate towards me. Taking a bite of one of the toasts, I tasted sugar, cinnamon, and a raisin or two. It all kind of stuck together on top of melted butter.

"Not bad," I said. "And when does an environmental scientist get time to work in the kitchen?"

"Got to eat just like cops. And I like to eat." He tore off a piece of toast and popped into his mouth. He had the habit of chewing and puffing out his cheeks at the same time.

"Cream?" He offered me a creamer that I rarely used.

"No." I watched him pour it into his cup, then add coffee.

"Learned this in Peru when I was studying there." He lifted his cup in a toast. I nodded.

"You've been busy." I wondered if his own kitchen looked like an archeological dig.

"I got to talk to you. No better way to talk than to eat first." He grinned and picked up another toast.

I put down my coffee cup. "Okay, Georgie, tell me what you've got."

He sipped loudly on the heavily creamed coffee, sloshed it around his puffy jowls and swallowed loud enough for me to hear. "It's about Nettleson."

"I figured that."

"I finally remembered who he was, and it's rather interesting." He grinned and stuck his hand out for the last piece of toast. I rested mine on top of his.

"Save it for dessert."

He shrugged his shoulders and smiled, trying to act embarrassed. Suddenly he sat up straight and became serious.

"He was in grad school for a while but dropped out to work for some kind of health food business. Raised some eyebrows really."

"Georgie, you're raising mine. Please go on."

"It's like this. You know those people who pull the hydrilla grass out of lakes and stuff? Well, Nettleson learned how to do that. Then he hooked up with this guy who pulls out the grass, dries it, crushes and presses it into pills. Sells the pills at health food stores."

"And what does it do for you—this hydrilla pill?"

"Supposed to be some kind of super vitamin. The grass contains all kinds of minerals and stuff. You can super dose yourself with a pill or two a day." Georgie took another loud sip of coffee and frowned. "Cold." He poured from the pot to warm his cup.

"And Sam Nettleson is helping harvest the stuff to make the pills?"

"Yeah. But, there is a problem, you see."

"No, I don't see. Show me."

"Nettleson runs around trying to harvest the stuff wherever he can. Now some places might be okay. But have you ever heard of Lake Samantha?"

I nodded. "It's near the air force base, about fifty miles south."

"Ever been in it?"

Realization began to focus in my brain. "I won't go in it. The base dumps all kinds of chemicals in there."

"About the biggest polluted lake around, right?"

"Yes, and he's harvesting from there?"

"Place is full of hydrilla. Now if you don't know, hydrilla exists to clean water. That's why they put it in aquariums. It's cleaning Lake Samantha, too."

"Surely there is some regulation on the stuff."

"Not to my knowledge. The FDA doesn't do anything to health food store stuff. Nobody knows if the grass soaks up the poisons, but Nettleson and his bosses are using the stuff as is for the pills."

"So theoretically at least, someone could be taking pollutants when he thinks he's taking vitamins?"

Georgie nodded and grinned. "If Nettleson is out this way, I'll bet he's harvesting from a water lane in the swamp."

I thought about meeting Sam on the forest lane and his boxes on the dolly. The water lane cut into the swamp was full of hydrilla. "I'll bet you're right." I poured Georgie another cup of coffee. "How'd you like to take a boat ride into the swamp, Georgie?"

"Georgie Porgie would like nothing better!"

We made a date to meet Vernon on a patrol boat the next morning. I didn't tell Tony. He would have questioned my sanity in bringing this scientist of weird proportions into the search for a missing teen's body. First, however, Georgie and I decided to check out maps of the area.

"So there is a holding pond here, not a flowing stream?" I bent over a map as a county geologist pointed out lines of waterways near Scrapper Creek.

"A while back, a developer thought he was going to build cabins back there. It's close enough to the creek and the river to be attractive to people who want a vacation cottage. He started to bull doze some trees, and, of course, had to dig a holding pond for the run off. The environmentalists stepped in and stopped the whole project. It's still in litigation, I think. Anyhow, the swamp—as swamps will do—closed in and grew all around this pond until it now looks like a water lane that goes nowhere. It's not too deep and stays filled with rain water."

"And hydrilla has about taken over."

"Shallow, lots of nutrients, warm water. Stuff loves a pond like this," he scratched his chin. "No matter how much grass is growing there, the place is still polluted."

"How's that?"

"The man who wanted to develop the place still owns it, and even though he can't build houses in the swamp, he is building them elsewhere. He's cut a road through there and carries waste material from other projects back there." The geologist shrugged and looked at Georgie. I thought I saw a grin forming at the edges of his mouth. It was like looking at a cartoon of a cat who had just ate the mouse.

"I guess it would take somebody with a camera to prove he's dumping, but, hey, my finger clicks as good as anyone's." Georgie smiled and wiggled his finger in the air.

"What kind of other projects?" I asked the geologist.

"Does stuff with upholstery material and has a few car mechanic shacks in the area."

I turned to Georgie who had begun rubbing his palms on his baggy pants. "You want to prove he's polluting, don't you?"

He leaned forward and smiled, revealing a crooked set of white teeth. "Don't you?"

CHAPTER ELEVEN

"Can I drive it?" Georgie Porgie bounced his round head like a beach ball. He took the seat next to Vernon, leaving me to sit behind the two. "I never did it before, and I'd like to try."

Vernon glanced back at me, his big warm grin absent and a look that said, "What the hell?" I shrugged.

"Sorry, sir," he spoke in the monotone police voice. "This is a patrol boat, and only authorized deputies can act as pilot. I could get into lots of trouble by turning over the wheel to you."

"Oh," Georgie poked out a bottom lip and scowled for about ten seconds. "Okay, let's go!" His mood suddenly up again, he sat up and grabbed the sides of his seat.

We had stashed Georgie's camera and other testing equipment in his canvas satchel underneath the back seats. With the tide in, Grandpa's Creek allowed us to move quickly into the landing at the end.

"This is where someone stole my canoe," I said. "Will they steal this boat, too?"

"Everything's locked and we've got a locater on it. Doubtful it would be stolen, except maybe by somebody a bit off his rocker." Vernon darted his eyes toward Georgie, then turned and helped me step off the boat and onto shore. He gave me a squeeze and a pat on the butt.

"Not in front of the kid," I said.

"If you hadn't told me he was a scientist, I would have said

Village Idiot," said Vernon as he gazed at Georgie picking up his bag and tripping toward the swamp.

"Wait!" I said. "You need to follow me."

"Oh, yeah." Georgie grinned and nearly fell into a bush as he let me cross in front of him. "I'm used to woods."

"Just watch your feet," said Vernon. "Rattlers like this neck of your familiarity."

Georgie giggled and snorted at Vernon's wit. If this man was going to help us, he'd have to show a lot more maturity by the time we got to the pond.

Molding leaves gave when we put our feet down on the path. It seemed the vegetation had crept in overnight and engulfed it like a blob in a sci-fi movie. A fecund odor rose off the swamp floor, the tell-tale signs of death and life occurring and recurring as we moved.

"There's Nettleson's trailer," I whispered as I turned back to face Georgie. He bumped into me, nearly dropping his satchel.

"Is he there?" Georgie stood on tiptoe, his head bobbing among the shoulder high bushes.

"No need to hide," I said as I moved toward the rusty structure. I knocked. Vernon joined me and went round back. Georgie stayed put in the trees.

"No one answers."

"And no one around back," said Vernon. "Those test tubes and boxes are still on the table. Like he never did anything with them."

"It's all a ruse," came a whisper from behind a tree. "I'm telling you, he's pulling hydrilla."

We trudged on, down the well traveled lane toward Jacob's house and turned off when we reached the pond path.

"Yep," said Georgie. He had dropped his backpack on the bank and leaned over the edge of the holding pond. He suddenly shoved one arm into the murky water and pulled out a handful of stringy hydrilla. "Just what I thought. Place is full of it. If we could see below the surface, we'd find spare places where he's pulled recently." He shook the vine-like grass from his arm and watched it drop back into the water. "That stuff will take root and grow overnight. Nettleson found himself a good racket."

"Is there anyway to test the stuff to see if it's full of pollutants?" I asked.

"Could be, but the industry isn't interested. Government neither."

"We'll take samples anyhow," said Vernon. He opened a plastic bag and scooped up hydrilla from the same location. "If it's not illegal, then why is he being so secretive about it?"

"Maybe we need to find out who he supplies," I said.

"I can do that!" Georgie began pulling sample bottles from his pack and filling them with water. "I need some from the middle." Before we could stop him, he walked into the pond until he was waist high in brown water. Stirring it up only brought about the putrid odors that had accumulated in still water. "Stuff is growing everywhere." Georgie pulled on his feet, then stood still and bent over to collect his samples. "Now get me back on shore." He walked, hands outward holding the samples like a balance beam. When he reached shore, Vernon pulled on his arms as I took the samples.

"Look at this stuff!" Georgie tugged on the vines that had wound round his legs. Instead of chunking it back into the pond, he shoved it into a bag he pulled from his backpack. "Wonder what Nettleson does to pull it up."

"Let's take a walk around," said Vernon as he headed off to his right. Going around the bank proved fairly easy. Someone had chopped back most of the bush. Only twice did Georgie lose his footing in the soft shoreline and nearly slide into the water. The swamp odor followed us as we rounded the pond and came closer to the offshoot creek.

"Not good this," said Georgie as he pointed to the creek water. "Hydrilla will move right into that water and fill up the passage."

"It's already there and in the river, too," I said as I watched clear water turn murky where someone had cut a passage from creek to pond.

"But not the pollutants," said Georgie. He put his head down, looking like a bloodhound in clothes, and followed a clearing that opened into the trees. "This is where they bring the stuff to dump, I'll bet!"

"And to pull the hydrilla," said Vernon. He knelt and pointed to tire tracks. "A truck has come through here. Big tires, like a swamp traveler." He moved to the side a bit. "And runner tracks, probably a back hoe. They use them to clean ponds, probably have some way of harvesting the hydrilla with the same machine."

"And why is Nettleson living here?" I asked. "If they can harvest the stuff and get it out, why do they need him?"

"To find the crops," grinned Georgie. "I bet he won't stay in that trailer too long, unless he's tracking down more sources right here in this swamp."

"Seems a lot of trouble when the grass grows fast and furious. Just dig a hole in your back yard and toss in a few strands. You've got a crop for a long time." I stood and listened to water birds cry out to each other. Were they eating from this cesspool?

"This is somebody's back yard," said Georgie.

"You know the owner?" asked Vernon.

"I know the dumper, but whether or not he's the actual owner," he shrugged. "I'll test this stuff if I can. They don't like us doing our own thing on university time, but I'll see what I can do." He lugged the back pack to his shoulders.

The three of us stood in the forest. Humidity embraced us and the horse flies swarmed around our heads. Georgie scratched some-where between his legs. Before anyone made a move, Vernon's pager sounded. A bird took flight just above us.

"It's Tony," said Vernon, closing his cell phone. "He wants us on the river pronto. Seems they've ID'd the skull you found in the sunken boat.

"Ooh!" said Georgie, his eyes lit up like fireflies under glass.

"No sir, you can't come," Vernon said. "When we pull into the landing, you head on out and do your tests. Tony's not likely to take you kindly."

Georgie pushed out his lower lip in his usual childish pout, then recouped his composure and grinned. "Okay!"

I got the front seat on the way back. Vernon winked at me, then glanced behind him. "You sure find the crazies, Luanne," he whis-pered.

"Found you, didn't I?" I winked back.

At the river landing, Vernon pulled in beside another patrol boat. Georgie was already up and moving onto the platform before Tony realized who we were. He gave the student a sharp glance and turned to us. "Giving people rides in boats?"

"Scientist," said Vernon. "He's with us." There was something about Vernon, a kind of *don't mess with my head* command when he dealt with Tony. Had I given him the same answer, he would have had me under questioning and even ranted and raved, until he needed me to dive somewhere.

"Let's meet under the tarp," said Tony. He turned his attention to a camper that had an extended overhang erected from the back. Underneath, there was a small table piled high with boxes and sur-rounded by several plastic chairs.

"Everybody here?" Tony looked out towards Vernon and me. We were joined by Loman and two scene techs along with two uniformed deputies.

"Marshall Long did some voodoo work in his lab and came up with a probable identity," he said, holding up a photo of the skull I had so gently escorted from its watery grave. It had been enlarged, making the eye sockets look like cave openings.

"Seems about a year ago, a local fisherman went missing. Said he was going into the Gulf for a little deep sea fishing. Never came back, and the Coast Guard never found a trace of the boat. He didn't have a family so nobody pushed looking for him, except a local lady who had befriended him over the years. She died about six months after the disappearance. Case has been sitting ever since."

"Sounds like this man never made it to the Gulf," I said.

Tony frowned. "Either that or when he came back from the trip, something happened."

"No sign of used fishing gear in his boat," I said.

Tony frowned again. "Okay, Luanne. Maybe he never made it out, but that's not the point. Cause of death was a bullet hole through the top of his head."

Tony wasn't going to admit that the man could have been forced at gun point to pull his boat into the creek rather head to the Gulf. He'd have to deal with the possibility, but he'd do it with his deputies.

I turned to Vernon. "He was inside the bilge. Could someone on deck have shot him from that point?"

Vernon winked and smiled. He knew the game. Irritate Tony, but be helpful. "Sounds reasonable to me."

"Does the skull have a name?" I asked.

"Otis Reynolds. A retired man of seventy when he went out last. The boat is registered to him, too. Marshall was able to extract some tooth DNA but we don't have a relative to compare it with right now. Got some deputies looking."

"Pasquin would know him," I said and immediately gasped. My fear that my friend was lost somewhere crept up my neck and for a moment I saw myself holding his Cajun skull in my hands. "Has anyone found him yet?"

"You want a search?" said Tony, whose normal nonchalance at finding swamp people was beginning to break. Pasquin had been gone too long.

"Yes," I said and closed my eyes. I would visit his swamp friends tonight. They had their own network and would know if he was away under his own power.

Tony gave Loman orders to organize a search for Pasquin, then told Vernon he was needed on another case. We parted company at my car door.

"Stay out of trouble," he said. He looked around him, avoiding the gaze of any deputies, leaned over and kissed my cheek. "I'll try to make it tonight."

I squeezed his hand. In another time I would have thrilled at the idea of a normal romp—if you could call what people did in their late forties romping—with Vernon. He made ugly things like murder disappear when he came for dinner and overnight. We had settled into a quite comfortable habit with each other. He kept his place; I kept mine. But the twain often met. This was not one of those times, however. The thought of a missing Pasquin sent chills over my heart and spurred an urgency to get looking.

Back at my place, I regretted not having my canoe. I also regretted not being able to call Pasquin and have him take me down the river. My Honda, small though it was, wouldn't make it on the narrow lane. The only thing to do was walk. I needed to get to Edwin's place. Edwin loved snakes and collected them. Sometimes he skinned them in his backyard and made belts from the hides. He knew the swamp and about nothing else. Pasquin often said he was a child-man, someone who had been born in a mosquito patch and still had the things buzzing in his brain. But Edwin loved Pasquin, and the old man trusted him. The snake collector would have to be my starting point.

I packed a bag with some cheese snacks, water, a pistol, and a cell phone, pulled on high boots and took off down the river bank path. It wasn't a clear path, and I often had to trudge through mud and sliding dirt to continue. All the while, I kept my eyes peeled for the water moccasins who soaked up sun rays on these banks. Alligators did the same, but they avoided humans if possible. I saw two of them slide into the water before I reached their dark-green, tough-hide bodies. I was comfortable and surefooted on the trail to Pasquin's house, but this one was longer and led into more primitive areas of the swamp. At one point, I stopped cold. The dreaded shake of rattles sounded in the air. I couldn't see the reptile, but his heat sensors told him where I was. After what seemed an eternity, the rattles stopped and the raspy sound of its body crawled away. That's when I caught a glimpse of the brown diamond shape slithering into the trees. I moved carefully, hoping the thing didn't have a mate.

Finally, I came to a clearing on a pristine part of the river. A crude tie-up was there, and Edwin's small motor boat rocked in the soft waves. The path, nearly invisible, led to his front porch. He had patched some of the rotting boards, so the structure was a mixture of ancient gray with fresh brown lumber. Edwin, himself, sat in a rocker. A snake hide rested in his lap along with a leather sewing basket. His head hung to the side, and he dribbled saliva onto his plaid shirt as he snored through an afternoon nap.

"Edwin!" I called from across the road. These swamp people kept pistols and rifles at their sides most of the time. I didn't want to risk getting shot by a startled child-man.

Edwin's head bobbed upward. He lifted one hand and scratched his hair, shoving it upward into a greasy spiked row.

"Luanne?" He grinned, looked down at the skin and carefully placed it on a table beside the rocker. "You want to come in?"

I took a deep breath. No, I didn't want to come in, but it looked like the best thing for the moment. I nodded.

"Good! I got some instant iced tea." He stood and held the screen door for me. "How come you didn't come by boat?"

"No boat to come in," I said. "My canoe was stolen and smashed." I gulped. "And Pasquin, we can't find him."

CHAPTER TWELVE

Edwin's house was a museum—a dead animal tribute to his knowledge of taxidermy. Stuffed reptiles dotted the walls. One huge oak snake, a brown spotted thing that must have been six feet long spanned the space above the hall door. To get into the back rooms, one had to walk under this monster. My blood ran cold.

"How do you live like this? Don't you have bad dreams?" I ducked as I went through the hallway door, even though the stuffed snake was dead and at least four feet above me.

"I like them," said Edwin. He scratched his uplifted hair and motioned me to follow him into a kitchen. A table for two had been placed at one end of the room. A large picture window gave anyone sitting there a view of the backyard—and all those cages, cutting table, and the clothesline that served as a drying spot for snake skins.

"You sit here and eat," I mused as I gazed out the window. If I focused my eyes on the cages, I could see brown and black and yellow bodies slither up and down the sides. "You watch reptiles while you have lunch."

"Yeah," said Edwin. He grinned now, like a school boy who had turned in the best science project. "And there's a guy over on the highway who's going to pay me to make belts and pouches out of snake skin."

"That's what you're sewing?" I started to sit in the chair, but the thought that something could be crawling on the floor made me stay put. Edwin handed me a glass full of a cold liquid. I gazed at the weak tea and nodded thanks.

"You want something made, too?"

"Oh, I think not, Edwin. Thanks anyway." I took the opportunity to set the tea glass on the little table and turn my back toward it. "I've come about Pasquin. We can't find him."

"You need him?" Edwin stood alert, his eyebrows rising to meet the upstanding hair. "I can help."

"I need you to help find him."

"But he goes all over the swamp. He ain't lost." Edwin's childish eyes grew large; fright that would never have surfaced at the sight of a rattlesnake showed itself now.

"He might be," I said. "Of course, he might not be, and that's where you come in. Can you and your swamp friends look for him?"

Edwin stood frozen silent for a moment. "Course I can." He put his own tea glass on the sink and dashed out the door. "I'm tired of sewing skins anyhow. I'll get right on it."

"And let me know what you find," I called after him as he collected his rifle and boat keys. "Hey! If you're taking a boat, how about giving me a ride to Fogarty Springs."

We sat in the small motor boat. The old engine sputtered into life and Edwin guided it into the main part of the Palmetto River. We would travel the short distance to a landing where I would get off in the tiny settlement named after my own ancestors. At the top of the landing sat the wood frame building that housed Mama's Table. A sign over the door read "the best fish house in the swamp."

"You want me to come back for you?" Edwin yelled as he revved the engine.

"No. I'll find a way back. Just be sure to report to me if you find him." I stood on the landing and watched him speed away. "And please find him," I whispered to the winds.

It wasn't dinner time, and Mama's Table had only three custom-ers. Two were disheartened fishermen who decided to eat the things rather than catch them. The third was Harry MacAllister. He waved to me from a side table when I entered.

"I was just getting ready to head to your place. I've got diving equipment in the boat." He toyed with a plate of fried oysters.

"You were going to dive on a full stomach, right?"

He stared at his plate, then swallowed hard. "Okay," he sighed. "I chickened out. Got this far on the river and just froze. Frankly, Luanne, I don't even know if I can put the tank on my back right now."

I nodded. "You ever try psychological counseling about this?"

He shrugged. "Sort of. Went once actually. His advice was to get back at it."

"Is it the fear of underwater bombs?" I leaned forward and placed a hand over the one he was using to fork an oyster.

"That, yes, and I keep seeing divers who have gone down, got in a panic, and never lived to see the surface again. And I see myself in their suits." He brushed his thick salt and pepper hair away from his forehead.

"Look, Harry. We can dive later today. Right now, I need your help in another way." I looked him in the eyes. "You have no fear of running your boat on the water, right?"

Harry's boat sat cleaned and sparkling at the landing. It was a long one that had places for scuba gear and other tools for an ar-cheology professor. His motor looked new, certainly more power-ful than Edwin's.

"I want to go to this spot where they found my stolen canoe, then see what kind of waterways stem from there."

Harry nodded, told me to point the way, and started the motor. The afternoon showed no signs of the usual summer monsoon.

We rode in clear air, passing a few fishermen, a couple of swimmers who took advantage of the cool waters over the side of their boats, and a girl scout troup who rowed in three canoes toward a campsite. Soon the manatee warning signs appeared and Harry slowed to a near crawl. By the time we found the creek turnoff, we barely moved through the thick hydrilla grass.

"You sure about this?" Harry said, some of the fear creeping back into his head.

"Positive. We've got a ways to go."

The creek, at points, almost disappeared in the thick tree growth in the water. Harry dodged between the trees, often backing up to free the motor of hydrilla. Once we saw a manatee, its cow-like body moving behind us as though the boat could be a mate. It finally went deep below, and I held my breath that it would not come back up and hit the propeller.

"Can't go much further, Luanne." Harry had taken an oar to push against some cypress roots.

"It's there!" The spot where the canoe had been dragged ashore was nearly obliterated, but a muddy scrape still existed between shore grass. "Can you tie up here?"

We made our way on foot up the muddy bank and across to where my bashed-in canoe had lain on its side. If Marshall had found anything like a fingerprint on it, hell, if he had even looked, I hadn't heard.

"Wonder what the purpose of smashing it was?" Harry looked about the area where sparse grass grew. We followed the line of notches Vernon had cut, passed the shallow water and headed through some trees. "Stream back here."

It was a stream, a moving one and deep enough for a row boat.

"I'd like to see where this goes," I said.

"No way to get my boat back here. We'll have to walk."

For about ten yards, the walking was hazardous on the soft shoulders of the creek bank. Then, a path showed up and turned abruptly through the trees. All the while, the creek ran alongside a heavy growth of oaks. When it widened, we realized where we were.

"The bridge," I said. "We're just down from Grandpa's Creek and where the sheriff is set up. The Hanover house is to our right.

"And just across the river is another creek," said Harry pointing to a water passage through the trees.

"Someone with the right kind of boat could travel all the way from inside the swamp on the west side, cross the river, and end up in more swamp on the east side."

"Looks like it," Harry gazed about him. "You know, that spot just beside the bridge is the most popular place for people to launch their boats." He pointed to a slanted drive that led from a make-shift dirt parking lot up beside the bridge to the water. Trucks with boat trailers waited in the lot for their owners to return from a day of water frolic.

We stayed for a moment, resting and drinking bottled water, then headed back into the swamp. "Let's try and walk next to the water," I said.

"Looks like someone has already done that," Harry pointed to muddy ruts that had been tamped out by human feet. "Could be a popular place for teens—hidden—if you know what I mean."

I looked at Harry. This man had once been my lover, warm and passionate. He would have taken advantage of such a hidden spot when we were dating a few years back. For a brief second I wondered if his other talents had been lost with his diving ones.

We moved through the ruts someone else had made along the bank, our left feet sliding into the mud, our right ones keeping the balance. At one point, I had mud up to my ankles and it was slowing me down. We came to a spot where mud eased into the water as though someone often put in a canoe here.

"I need to get this boot off," I said, finding a patch of grass to sit on where I could stick my foot into the water.

"Nice clear spring in this area," said Harry as he joined me. We pulled off our boots and soaked our feet in the cool running water. "Probably some underground aquifer in the area."

Harry leaned back, his arms folded behind his head. "You see a snake nibble on my toes, let me know." He laughed and somewhere in that grin and those wrinkles around his eyes, I saw the old Harry, relaxed, at peace with his world. It didn't last long. He moved his head away from an interfering sun ray and turned silent at the same time.

"Harry?" I glanced to see him staring into the water.

"What the hell is that?" He didn't sit up, just reached one hand across his face and pointed to the dark water.

In the middle of the creek, at least two feet below the surface, something waved about. At first glance, it could have been a hand-kerchief, or an abandoned towel tossed there by some teen who went for an *au naturel* swim. But first glances often prove nothing more than alarm buttons. It looked more like white hair to me.

"Oh, God!" I whispered to the winds and said a prayer that it wasn't Pasquin's white cockatoo hair. "My God!"

"Luanne?" Harry stared up at me.

I dived into the water. It didn't matter that my clothes could pull me down in the currents. I didn't care that hydrilla might surround me. I held my breath and moved through the creek like a frightened frog running from a gator.

It was a man all right, and an elderly one. I pulled on an overall strap of one shoulder. He didn't move up, only backward. Holding my breath, I looked directly into the lined face.

"It's Jacob Halley," I yelled as I tread water. "Get in here and help me get him out."

My heart banged against my ribs in absolute relief that it wasn't Pasquin, but a thorn stuck in my brain. If Jacob was here, Pasquin could be, too.

"Luanne," Harry stood on the bank, hesitant, his gaze begging. "Shouldn't we call the police?"

"Help me, Harry!" I screamed at him.

It worked. He jumped into the water and swam to me.

"I can't pull him up. Something has him. Maybe hydrilla."

We went down, holding our breath as long as possible. On the second dive, we found the source. A crude rope was tied around his ankles and attached to a cement block.

"You'll have to call Tony," Harry said as he panted on the bank. He lay in mud, gasping.

"The phone is in my backpack," I said. I reached for it, and while waiting for an answer, I saw Harry's gasps as fear more than fatigue. If he keeps seeing death in water, I thought, how will he ever get over this?

The swamp, calm most of the time except for the occasional gator snack or bird squawk, filled up with police crime scene material. They came from both sides, tying up near Harry's boat and boating in from the bridge. Tony had brought along diving equipment for me. Another diver, new to the force, went down with me to use the metal mesh carrier. I had never had to do this before. Tony always said I wasn't a real deputy and couldn't touch the bodies. But he had no one else today. One department diver and me. Harry stood by, helping with the tanks.

The cement block barely did the job of holding the body down. It wasn't heavy. The other diver strapped the body into the basket, turned it over and pulled it to the bank. I followed, carrying the block still attached to the ankle rope like some midwife with a still-born umbilical attached.

On shore, there was an attempt to set up an area to work. Marshall Long had traipsed his large self through the swamp from a boat that stopped at the head of the creek. Sweat poured from his large head and plastered his hair to the round face. With the lab coat flying around him, he looked like Nero ready to light the fires.

"Drag him here," he ordered the deputies who pulled on the body basket, their feet digging into mud and nearly toppling one into the river. They deposited Jacob on a tarp that had been spread across the swamp floor. The cement block lay two feet away, still attached like a satellite to his feet. He wore no shoes.

Marshall's rotund body moved around the tarp until he found a place to poke with his gloved hands. He examined the half-closed eyes that stared into a vacuum, then the neck by pulling back the collar of the plaid shirt. After going down the front of the man, he gave the order to turn him over. Two gloved techs did this as easily as rolling a log.

"There's your cause of death," he said. He had found a ragged spot where the skull met the spinal cord, just above the overalls. The hole made a path and came out through the shirt near the wind pipe. Peeling back the overalls, Marshall pointed to the hole, cleaned now by pristine spring water.

"Shot from the back?" I felt my blood run cold. Was someone killing off swamp people?

I pulled off my tank and handed it over to Harry. His hands trembled when he took it, and I had to help him lift it into the equipment boat. He looked at me, sheepishly, but said nothing.

Tony and Loman joined us. "You keep finding bodies, Luanne," said Loman, "and we're going to arrest you." He tried to laugh. Tony ground his teeth, his olive skin beginning to redden. Harry sat on the ground, sweating and breathing hard.

"Give him something to drink," I said to a deputy. Bewildered, the man handed Harry a soda.

"Got any candy?" He added with a nervous laugh. "Death kind of makes a man hungry."

For a brief second, I sounded a question in my brain, "a man?"

"We got trouble, it seems," said Tony. "Two old men shot. Both found in river creeks. Year apart." He turned up dirt with the highly polished toe of his shoe. "Anybody got any ideas?" He breathed heavily.

"No ideas, but another worry," I said as I toweled my hair. "Where the hell is Pasquin?"

All the men turned to me, their voices silent. They all knew what I knew. The old man, Pasquin, had always been the one to find them or some other person they had lost in the swamp. No one ever expected to be looking for him.

"Hey!" Marshall Long's voice boomed into the swamp over the voices of deputies and scene techs. His large hand pointed into the forest where something made foot sounds that moved away from us. "I could swear a naked woman just ran through those trees."

CHAPTER THIRTEEN

"Alice?" I said under my breath. "She's a long way from Scrapper Creek."

Tony glanced my way.

"You probably saw a young deer," he said.

"Look, Mr. Big Honcho. I'm a medical examiner. I know things when I look at them, and that was no deer. Not unless it ran on two legs and had a long gray main."

"It's Alice," I said. "I'll have a look."

"Take a deputy," said Tony as though resigned to giving in to crazies. I nodded and headed into the trees. He must have made a motion, because one of the uniforms followed me.

"You know where you're going?" The deputy, a rookie, all of maybe twenty-five, jerked thorny vines from the brown material that made up his neatly pressed shirt.

"Do you?" I kept moving, trying to follow the broken limbs and muddy tracks.

"Frankly, no. I'm not a country boy." He swore under his breath and stopped to wipe mud from the side of his shoe.

"Place is full of puddles. Snakes, too." I stopped abruptly and turned to him. "You did bring your gun?"

He stood white faced, then touched the holster on the side of his hip. "Sure."

We arrived at what might have served as a wild hedge. Bushes grew to our shoulders and formed a barrier. The deputy shrugged as he tried to find an opening.

"Here's some mud on the ground," I said. "She could have gone this way." I parted the limbs.

"Listen!" The young man said, and his hand traveled again to his hip.

In the dead silence we heard what could have been a faint humming. It grew louder then faded and grew louder again. I pushed on the bushes, scratching the backs of my hands, and peered into a space that led down an incline into a clearing. It appeared to be an old sinkhole area that had long since covered up in grass; no bushes or trees grew in the space. It couldn't have been more than six feet wide.

I pointed to the opposite side where more tall bushes grew. A dress hung there, and a pair of battered sandals sat on the ground beneath it. The humming came and went with Alice's turns. Like radar, she spun around in a steady rhythm. She had a towel in her hands and moved it up and down her back as she spinned.

"Little Mary knew what to do. Little Mary grew and grew." She had stopped humming and sang the words to some made-up song. "Little Mary tricked the crew. Little Mary knew what to do." Her nonsensical rhymes drifted into a series of "lu-lu-lu-lu" as she made her turns.

She twirled until she became dizzy, then sat bare-butt on the grass. Pulling on her long hair, she wound it upward, forming a turban with the towel and tucking the ends firmly against her head. The towel pulled up the skin, and suddenly the old woman looked years younger. The deputy and I glanced at each other, embarrassed that we were staring at her nakedness. Alice's arms and legs looked remarkably strong for an old lady. Running through the swamp keeps you fit, I thought.

"Should we disturb her?" the deputy whispered. He didn't whisper very well. Alice's turbaned head rose suddenly like a dear who hears the bobcat stalk the bushes. She darted upward, pulled on the dress and shoes and shot into the forest on the other side of the incline.

"Tony can find her later," I said. "He may need to ask her some questions about seeing anybody out here." The deputy stared at me. "Well, if you want to run after her, go ahead, " I added. He shook his head.

Laughter about an old woman running naked and wild in the woods helped to relieve some of the gruesomeness of seeing Jacob's old body lifeless on the tarp. But I couldn't laugh. It was Pasquin's body I saw lying there.

"I want to go the distance of this creek," I said. No one asked why, and again Tony ordered the deputy to follow. Harry begged off, saying his leg had started to ache again.

I positioned myself on the edge of the bank and walked, staring into the forest then into the water. Several times, old logs bobbed in the currents and I stopped to investigate. Once, a water bird darted suddenly out of the water and startled me. I fell backward into the deputy who fell into the mud. "Are you a country boy, yet?" I asked as I watched him try to remove the wet stuff from his uniform. He grunted instead of answering.

The creek finally went underground. No doubt it again emerged somewhere and flowed into the lane from the main river. The aquifers, seen and unseen, do funny things in the state of Florida. The entire area is a giant honeycomb that occasionally spews water to the surface. More than one diver has lost his life trying to find the doors to these underground synapses.

"No Pasquin," I whispered as I breathed in the hot damp air.

Once Marshall Long had transported Jacob's body off in a patrol boat, the scene techs finished their work and handed the area back to Tony. His tense jaw worked, the only sign of anything out of place. The man didn't sweat.

"Okay, where does this Alice woman work?" He rose on his toes just like Loman who stood next to him. They reminded me of geese whose necks bowed and stretched.

"Last I heard, she cleaned rooms at the Ocean Pine Motel, but they had to let her go. Actually," I sighed, "she cleaned for Jacob, too."

Tony gazed at me, his black eyes unblinking. "All the more reason to question her."

"Anyone know where she lives?" I asked.

There was no answer. Tony decided we'd head for the Ocean Pine and begin there.

"What about looking around that clearing?" I said. "How did she get out of here?"

Tony stopped, his jaw clinching. He hated it when I did things like this. One of his men could say it and he'd go along. But not the woman, the one who wasn't even a sworn deputy.

"We can check it out," said Vernon. He usually stepped in when he saw his boss at a loss for words, at moments when pride was about to overrule reason.

The entire crew headed for their boats or walked the path back to the river. Vernon and I took off through the bushes to the clearing.

"You protect that bastard, don't you?" I teased.

"That bastard is in a position that needs protecting," he said. "He's the boss, and believe me, he's better than some others around the department."

"What's his beef with me?" I pushed through an opening Vernon had made by parting the limbs.

"Just ol' boy stuff," said Vernon. "He comes from a long line of Cuban machismo and redneck bravura. You're the modern woman; he prefers a sweet Magnolia." Vernon popped me on the rear.

"Sweet Magnolias don't dive in caves, and they damn sure don't get pats on the rear." I pinched his side.

"Bet they did after they took off all those petticoats."

"Tony needs me," I said.

"He knows that, but he's got to make sure you know he could do without you."

"Could he?"

"Of course not, and he knows that, too. You see how the man is a seething ground of contradictions. And when you put logic into the picture, well, the ego thing just swells up like a tick full of blood."

We reached the clearing and eased through the bushes to the incline. Edging into the bottom, we found a small pile of rocks with pine needles sticking up where they had been placed in a circle. In between the needles, Alice had placed tiny wildflowers, some purple, some yellow. The area in the bottom was damp where water had accumulated in a recent rain. The woman's footprints had made a bare space in a circle around the rock shrine. More muddy prints headed up the opposite bank to where her dress had been hanging. She had put on her shoes sometime before leaving the area, because the muddy prints ended at the top of the incline.

"The original nature witch," Vernon said as he tried to follow the prints. "Let's go this way. It looks the easiest to push through the bushes.

He was right. Once out of the rim of bushes, we found a trail that led right to the end of the creek. Several boats tied up here, including canoes and row boats. There was no sign of Alice.

"This is how she gets in and out," said Vernon. "Bet she's been up and down that creek lots of times."

I looked at Vernon. "Are you thinking there may be more of her in this than Tony suspects?"

"She's the village idiot as far as most people around here are concerned. Can the idiot commit crime? What's the motive?"

"There's another idiot, Vernon. A male. Barley Ben. Remember him?" I said it with contempt, silently condemning him of doing the same macho thing Tony did. "Besides, I don't think Alice is an idiot. Crazy maybe, but no idiot."

Vernon reached for my hair and pulled me close. "Let's go find some idiots," he whispered and bit my ear lobe.

We drove through the lowlands of palmetto scrub and sand to reach the Ocean Pine Cafe and Motel that backed up against the bay. A few cars with boats trailing behind pulled into the cafe lot and emptied themselves of sunburned children and fussy adults. They all scrambled inside, most heading to the rest rooms before sitting down to plates of fried shrimp. A trail of beach sand across the floor would track their movement. The motel's vacancy sign was on but the red light barely showed in the bright sunlight. Not a single car was parked in front of the tiny row of rooms.

"Times aren't good," said Vernon. "Economy is keeping everybody at home."

"Economy and the fear that some terrorist buzzard is going to blast Disney World into the clouds."

Vernon sighed and made some breathy comment about the world being a different place now. "Must not have been too good years back, either," he said and pointed to several crumbling bungalows behind the motel rooms. They dotted the landscape among the tall palms and low palmetto. At one time, someone had boarded the windows, but the wood had rotted and now each building stood open to the insects and reptiles of a Florida forest.

"Good place for a homeless person," I said.

"And there have been a few, I'm sure." Vernon tugged my elbow and we entered the cafe.

Calvin, the young man who hired out at Mama's Table, was clearing dishes.

"You must like this work," I said.

"Hate it. But, I need the money and if my parents are paying somebody else, they can't give me the tuition I need." He shoved a bowl of shrimp hulls onto his tray and headed toward the kitchen. "Somebody will be with you in a minute."

"Come back yourself," said Vernon.

When Calvin returned, he had changed his ketchup smeared apron for a clean one. "This isn't about food, is it?"

I shook my head. "We want to know about Alice."

"Crazy Alice?" He made a half laugh, then rolled his eyes. "She's crazy all right. Used to do a decent cleaning job around here, but she got too chummy with the guys. Now she ain't no twenty-year-old doll, and the guys didn't much like it. We let her go." Calvin snapped his fingers in the air.

"Where does she live?" asked Vernon.

Calvin shrugged. "Not sure. There's a rumor her old man left her a swamp shack, but it's probably rotten by now. Oh, and we did find her snoozing in one of the bungalows out back once. Had an empty bottle of bourbon lying across her belly." He stopped and grinned. "Her naked belly. She had pulled off all her clothes and was sleeping on the floor."

"Woman seems to have an aversion to clothes," said Vernon. "Mind if we look around back there?"

Calvin shrugged and shook his head. "Just be careful of snakes. They curl up in the corners and under some of the stuff lying around back there."

Calvin showed us out the back door, one that led directly into a patch of weeds under two giant palms. "Mind if I borrow this?" Vernon took a broom whose bristles had rotted down to two inches. He held it upside down and poked about the weeds before we stepped. Only two well fed frogs hopped about, a sure sign no snakes lay in wait.

The first bungalow was nothing more than a hut now. Windows on all sides were completely open to nature. A rusting bed spring lay in the middle of the cement floor but there was no evidence of a dresser or other amenities that a tourist would expect after a long ride on a two-lane highway. Vernon pushed on the door. It moved, then fell flat into the room. On one side, a niche with a rod still stood waiting for a visitor to hang his shirts. Next to it was a tiny doorless room that had been a bathroom. The sink and toilet had long since disappeared into flea market heaven.

"Must have been a great place once," said Vernon. He poked the corners even though we could see nothing rested there.

"I remember them from my high school days," I said. "Lots of people came down here for the fishing and swimming in the bay. And these cabins housed a ton of teens during spring break."

Vernon laughed. "Bet a lot of babies sired here, too."

We moved on to another cabin and another until we reached the last one that still stood with four walls and a roof.

"They put them in a row along a path," said Vernon, "not lined up parallel to the highway." He turned and faced the bay. "I'll bet it was a pleasure to spend the night here. Breeze off the bay, all this quiet."

"Certainly didn't provide air conditioning back then." I imagined the feel of the night heat closing in as I lay on sheets soaked in my own sweat. Only luck and bay winds would keep out the mosquitoes. By morning, I would be as wet as if I had taken a dip in the ocean—and just as salty. "And I'll bet that's why this place dried up. People have to be cool nowadays."

Some leaves had blown into this last cabin. They lay in moldy stacks against the streaked walls. Vernon touched one pile and the inevitable happened. A large black snake moved into a curl, his head raised and tongue darting.

"Okay, sir, we don't need to see this one." Vernon pushed back on me and we headed away.

"No signs of a Crazy Alice here," I said. "Not even a ceremonial rock mound."

"She's got to live somewhere," said Vernon. "I'll get somebody to check the shelters and homeless stations. Could be she roves."

When we headed back to the main motel, we saw a pot-bellied man come out of one of the rooms. He staggered a bit, and spilled beer from his can. He looked familiar.

"Isn't that Hanover's diver?" I asked.

Vernon nodded. "Chalker. And he might be another body down there with Tommy if he keeps on drinking that stuff." We watched while the man loaded his truck with scuba gear. "Seems a little late to be going for a dive."

At twilight, we returned to my house in the swamp by the Palmetto River. This was my cocoon, my haven amid creatures who could poison me in a second. My swamp dog was nowhere when we walked onto the screened porch.

"Plato must have another spot to hole up," said Vernon.

"He's a smart little cookie," I said. "Roams the swamps, then gives me company when he needs it. I'll put out some food."

The night closed around us as we sat on the porch and used iced tea to wash down some roast beef sandwiches. Behind us, we could hear the air conditioning system click on to cool the house.

"Wasting your money," said Vernon. He sat in the dark of the porch. I could hear him but only make out an outline in the absence of light.

"It's my money." I rested my head on the back of the rocking chair. This was the life, listening to frogs strike up a loud chorus and a water bird in the distance. I knew the river was out there just beyond the drive that I could no longer see. I knew the swamp was there, its gators and snails and anhinga birds doing the natural survival gyrations. On my safe porch, I embraced it.

Vernon planned to stay the night. My lover, friend, and almost-guru had been a part of my life for years now. We were comfortable with each other; he was another part of the natural scene around me; I was grateful.

"You ready to go in?" I said.

"Thought you'd never ask," he whispered back.

The cool sheets welcomed two hot bodies whose rhythms made use of years of swimming training, stroking, gliding, awash in each other, until the energy was spent and sublime sleep overcame us both.

Sometime between limbo and nirvana, I thought I heard the familiar whiz and whine of a motor boat rushing down the river. Later, I was sure I heard the sound of the telephone next to my ear.

"It's for you," I said and passed the receiver to a drowsy Vernon who always came alert at the sound of a phone in the night. "Tony."

"I'm off," Vernon said as he put down the phone. "You get some sleep."

"What's happened?" I half rose off the disarrayed sheets.

"Late night boaters found a body in the bay. Probably drowned." He turned to me when I gasped. "Tony says he's no white-haired Pasquin."

I nodded, my throat too choked to speak.

"Go back to sleep." He pulled on his shirt and pants and tramped down the stairs. I heard the front screen slam and his car start.

Sleep evaded me for nearly an hour. Then it appeared in fits where I'd awaken suddenly, turn over and doze again. In my stupor I heard the pat of rain against the window pane and worried that Vernon would be swimming in danger of lightning. The pats came harder and louder, and much too even. I rose and pulled back the yellow curtain material.

"Edwin!" The silly face with his hair standing straight up grinned back at me. I had the feeling of a body floating in air like some vampire ready to be welcomed inside. I pulled up the window. "How in the world did you get up here?"

"Got your ladder from your carport," he said. "I knocked on the front door, but nobody came. I been rapping on this window a long time."

"It had a screen on it." I leaned into the humid night air to see the screen lying at the bottom of the ladder.

"Had to remove it to get to the glass." He grinned again, and I groaned. How easy it would be for a thief or worse to walk right into my cocoon.

"Why?"

"You got to come with me," he whispered and looked about the darkness. "It's Pasquin."

CHAPTER FOURTEEN

Edwin's tiny motor boat rested at the end of my landing. I had pulled on jeans, a tee shirt, some high boots, and followed him in a run to the boat. He held it steady while I took the spare seat.

"It's going to be kind of a long ride," he said.

"Where are you taking me?"

"Place called Portu Landing. The old man said to bring you." Edwin revved the engine and guided it slowly into the deep center of the river.

"You mean Pasquin. Is he all right?"

Edwin put a finger to his lips and looked about him. "He said to make sure nobody but you knows."

I nodded and decided talking wasn't the best thing to do with Edwin's general wit. He needed full attention to driving a boat down a hydrilla-filled river in the middle of the night. He had a guide light in the front and a small light on a pole near the motor.

"I heard a boat racing down this way earlier tonight. Was that you?"

Edwin shook his head, a bouncing circle of shadows in the boat light. The moon was not there tonight.

I leaned back and let the slight spray hit my face, a cooling effect. The boat slowed down for grassy areas then sped up again. When, after nearly half an hour, we entered the manatee danger area, Edwin slowed to a near stop. In this darkness, we wouldn't see the animals if they came near the propeller. He edged through the brackish water near the crime scene, its tarps lit up through the night. Passing under the bridge, he headed for the open waters of the bay. Just at the point where it began, he made a turn and curved around the shoreline. The water was deep here and the grass sparse. He sped up. The sound of the engine moaned on and on until I nearly dozed off. We had been several miles down shore before he turned into another creek area.

"Where are we?" I whispered.

"Portu Landing," he said. "Watch down that way for a camp." He pointed into the darkness.

Trees bowed over this creek and dragged moss across my head more than once. I had the eerie feeling that a snake was going to drop in and join us at any moment. The blackness was impenetrable. It was like swimming in a cave, the only light immediate and unrevealing of what was just beyond its dim glow.

I heard voices before I saw a fire. They sounded like swamp ghosts luring us into their night dimension. At the end of the creek, an ancient wooden landing loomed in the murky light. Two boats were already there; one was the familiar vessel that had transported me from alligator farms to Mama's Table. "Oh, God!" I sighed.

"He's right there," said Edwin.

"Pasquin!" I helped pull the boat toward the tiny dock. I watched the old man lift his straw hat in salute from his seat on a fallen tree trunk. Another man, his equal in age, poked at the campfire.

"You planning on getting out of there?" The familiar voice reached my ears. I had resumed my seat in the boat, my eyes full of tears.

Edwin helped me out and I dabbed at my eyes with the backs of my hands. "You old bastard! Where have you been?"

He patted the fallen trunk, motioning for me to join him. "Had to keep quiet for a few days," He said. "You want some coffee?

Gavi makes a good outdoor brew." He pointed to the old man who grinned until he showed pure gum and no teeth. He had cut his hair into a short buzz so that the gray and black stubble that grew there formed patterns. I thought of crop circles. He rose and handed me a tin cup full of steaming black liquid.

"I done got her," said Edwin as he joined us, taking another cup from Gavi. "Had to crawl up her wall to do it."

"I'll ask about that later," chuckled Pasquin. He pulled his straw hat from his knee and placed it on his head. He took it off again and looked at it. "This is what got me running."

"Your hat?" I sipped the black liquid and swallowed hard. It was get-up-and-walk caffeine.

"Jacob's hat," he said and suddenly looked sad. "Swamp vine says he's dead."

"Yeah, shot," I said. "The hat?"

"That day we went looking in his house. I saw two things: his straw hat on the nail on the wall and his swamp boots on the floor right underneath. But I didn't see Jacob. Not inside nor outside the house. I got this feeling things weren't right. For him to go outside without the hat and boots, well, that's just not what a swamp hermit might do."

"And you came here?" I looked around. Beyond the light of the fire sat a tiny camper/trailer that must have been twenty years old.

"Been sleeping in that thing, along with Gavi for too many nights now." Pasquin chuckled. "Had a companion the whole time. But he done run off tonight. He'll be back before dawn. Always is." Pasquin looked up at me and smiled.

"Plato? So that's where he's been. I thought maybe the swamp had got him after all."

"Jumped in the boat with me when I stopped at one place and stayed the whole time."

"Good old swamp dawg, that one," said Gavi who sipped loudly on his cup. "Knows his way around gators and snakes."

"We're a long way from Fogarty Spring, aren't we?" I put the cup on the ground. If I drank anymore, I'd be awake for a week.

"Not even in the same county. Your daddy owned a bait and tackle place not far from here." Pasquin pointed into the vague area of the trees. "Good fishing, but not a place where tourists come."

The night surrounded us in mystery. What eyes from what creatures could be watching and listening to us right now? I watched Edwin slide off the trunk and rest his head against it. When he began to doze off, Pasquin took the cup from his hand and nodded to Gavi.

"I'll just go see the man," said Gavi, his way saying he'd take a leak somewhere back in the trees.

"Where were you, old man?" I gulped back the tears again. "You had me worried sick."

"Swamp vine had word on me," he said, referring to the old men and women who had inhabited these woods along with its gators, snakes, panthers, and insects, not to mention the "haints" they believed roamed on top of the river mists. They had ways of getting word to each other, of finding lost ones during troubled times. Pasquin would run to them if he thought he was in danger. "Gavi says I'm always welcome here. Been eating fish nearly everyday, Luanne. Little different from Mama's Table, but good just the same."

I sighed. "Don't start with the trivia, old man. Tell me why you ran. It wasn't only because you sensed danger. You would have gone to the sheriff if it was only that."

He chuckled, picked up a stick and gouged the dirt in front of his foot. "This old brain got to remembering something. Too far back for details. But, I got to saying Crazy Alice's last name over and over, and something sparked. Decided to talk to Gavi and some others who come here to camp. Found out some stuff about old Alice Calder." He chuckled again. "There's a reason she's crazy."

Gavi came back to the fire as if on cue and tossed on another log. "You want me to tell the story?" he asked as he poured himself another cup. I wondered if the man was nocturnal.

Pasquin took off his hat and tipped it in the man's direction.

"Calder family been in these parts a long time. Had this old farm house about two miles back that way." He pointed a thumb over one shoulder. "Farmed a little, but mostly rented out boats to weekend fishermen. Did okay. Old man Calder had four girls. He kept saying how they weren't no good to help out on a farm or with boats. Wasn't true, of course. All four knew how to run them boats. I'm getting ahead of myself. When the girls was little, Calder got called off to war. Got into some heavy fighting in France, but he come back okay. Not okay like before. He'd got mean and bossy, kind of like one of his commanding officers might have been. Barked orders to them girls and his poor wife. The wife didn't last long. Died of something or the other. The older girls were tall thin things. Old Calder called them his fillies, pretty horses. They got married quick out of school. Kind of made the old man happy 'cause he then had some male help. Didn't last. They took off and left him alone with the youngest, Alice." Gavi picked up a piece of kindling wood and scratched his back. "Alice wasn't a filly. She tended toward short and plump, and the old man called her his little moo cow. Now that might have been okay done in jest as a little kid, but don't no female want to be called a cow. Then she wasn't young anymore. At least not what her old man thought young enough for marriage. She had a beau or two, but nobody panned out. She got jobs in some tourist spots down on the bay, but nothing you'd call a career. She had to stay home and take care of her old man who had took to drinking big time. Probably been doing it since he came back from the war but nobody knew it until he passed out on a river bank. I found him once right there on that dock, bourbon bottle in hand." Gavi pointed toward the landing. "When he got sloshed he'd talk about how his daughter couldn't find her a man and he was going to have to leave the house to her since she had no other means of support. He'd cry in his whiskey about that old run-down place that was going to be sold in order to support an old maid daughter. Alice would giggle and say, 'Oh, hush, Poppa.' She was hurting. You could see it in her eyes. She had this long black hair and great big brown eyes—cow eyes, her papa said. They'd just float in all that hurt."

"You about to get to the point?" said Pasquin.

Gavi shot him an irritated look. "Old Calder was proud of his days in WW2. Had lots of souvenirs, including two pistols. He liked to practice with them when he first came back. Taught the girls how to use them."

"He taught Alice?" I asked.

Gavi nodded. "Later on, when the other girls were gone, and he was into drinking most of his days away, he took out those pistols. Cleaned both of them. Loaded one. Went outside and blew a hole in his head. Splattered his brains all over the oak tree in his front yard. Alice found him."

"She got a little more crazy after that," added Pasquin. "Kept saying if only he'd had a son-in-law to help out. Don't know what he would have helped with, maybe bring the old man his drinks."

"She all of sudden sold the land and moved off somewhere. Nobody knew just where. Then we started hearing about a Crazy Alice over near Tallahassee and figured she'd taken up there."

"She made enough money to live for a while," said Pasquin. "Man that bought her place just lets it sit."

"Who bought it?" I asked.

"Man called Hanover," said Gavi. "Hear tell he's lost his son in a boating accident."

"Looks that way. Never found his body, however." I peered into the fire, its embers shooting up and dissolving in the humidity a few feet above the flames. Did Alice know Hanover owned her old place?

"Well," drawled Gavi, "this old swamp might never cough him up." He poked the fire as though he had nothing else to do. "Seen it lots of times. Young kid decides to go swimming. Got a little beer in him. Gets caught on underwater vines and nobody sees him again. Then along comes a big storm and bones get washed up on shore— six, seven years later." He tossed his wooden stick onto the fire. "Old man Hanover might as well give up on that boy."

"You ain't finished the tale," said Pasquin, his hat slapping against his thigh beat out his frustration with the slow story.

"Not much else, except we heard, off and on over the years, how Alice would grab hold of some good-looking man and tell everybody she'd found her man. She'd grin and scare the fellow half to death. Everybody else got a kick out of it, laughed at her. She always thought they were laughing with her, kind of congratulating her on her find." Gavi chuckled. "The fellows she grabbed had to pull all kinds of tricks to get away from her. Word got around that a good way was to say, 'Alice, let me go get you a flower,' and she'd let go of his arm. Man would dart around back of a house or tree and just disappear." Gavi's face turned down and his swarthiness took on a shadow quality. "Something happened one time. She grabbed some young punk who didn't know what to do. Kid jerked away and called her a beefy old cow and to keep her filthy hands off him. Alice didn't like that. Those big eyes of hers went fire red, and she said right then and there, 'I'll be back for you!' And off she ran.

This was over by a bath house at the public campground. The kid hung around with his buddies, laughing and joking about the fat lady and what she might want to do with a young stud. Didn't take long to see what she planned to do with him. In come Alice with them two war guns of her daddy's and aimed both of them at the man. His buddies took off flying, leaving him standing right in the corner of the room. Other fellows were changing into bathing trunks and were in all stages of undress. They took off, too." He laughed and shook his head. "Alice pulled one of the triggers and a bullet hit the wall. Left a hole in the cement. That kid didn't stick around for the next one to go off. He high-tailed it to the river, jumped in the first boat he saw and sped into the trees. Cops were called but Alice had done run into the swamp by then. Nobody ever found her guns."

Gavi's tale faded away. He leaned back, grabbed another piece of wood and tossed it on the fire.

"She's got something on her mind about men," said Pasquin. "Poor old soul."

I looked at my watch. Four in the morning. "It's going to be dawn soon. Could you take me to see the old Calder place?"

Gavi turned his head slowly, then glanced at Pasquin. A tiny glint appeared in his eye and the corners of his mouth turned up. "Old Cajun there said you'd put me to work." He stood up. "Come on, then." He walked to the landing and pulled on the boat tied next to Pasquin's.

Pasquin still sat by the fire, his arms folded across his chest and his straw hat over his face. He wasn't asleep and called after us. "I'll have breakfast ready when you get back."

Portu Landing was strictly a stopping off place on a narrow but deep creek. There were no other places to pull in and no houses, not even a fish hut. At the end, we tied the boat to a tree limb and climbed ashore. The scrub was thick and wild, and huge pine and oak trees mingled as though they were crayons that would color everything dark. "Not much traffic through here, right?"

"None except deer, bear, and hunters. Got a walk ahead of us. You okay?"

As soon as I nodded, he turned and began to walk. I tagged along, trying to step where he stepped and to grab the limbs before they came slamming into my face. He didn't hold things but expected me to anticipate the dangers. I had two nasty nettle scratches on my hands by the time we reached a grassy clearing. The trees thinned out here, revealing a green, splotchy carpeting around bricks that once formed a chimney. A few stones marked the outline of the original big house. From the size of the foundation, it must have been a large, two-story affair.

"I'll bet you could see the river from the second floor," I said.

"Was a grand old house. Nothing left now." Gavi kicked a few stray bricks back toward the fireplace.

"No one comes here?" I headed for a pile of river stones.

"Not that I know of. No paths through the lanes or anything to signal a visitor."

"Except this," I said and pointed to a circular pile of stones with a few dead flowers poked between them. "Alice hasn't forgotten her ancestors."

Gavi gazed down at the little memorial on the space where a floor once stood. "Funny thing," he said and scratched his chin. "She put one of these right in the spot where her daddy killed himself. I'll never forget it." He looked far into the sky as though he could see the big house, complete and menacing. "Few rocks with flowers stuck in between."

"We saw her dancing and singing around something like that," I said. "Something about Mary knowing what to do."

"Mary?" Gavi asked, his dark eyes staring at me.

"That's the name she used. Anyone you know?

"It's her name—Mary Alice Calder."

Pasquin stirred sliced sausages in the pan over the outdoor grill. The aroma of spiced pork sat on the humid air and stimulated appetites. Gavi poured water into the coffee pot and made another strong brew. I sliced cantaloupe.

"So you think Alice may have gone after Jacob?" I pushed a hot sausage into my mouth. The spices hit the back of my throat like a blow torch. Pasquin handed me a full cup of coffee.

"She knew him before. He's one she thought she might marry years ago. He wasn't interested, of course. Too much to take on with her daddy. He went off somewhere and didn't see her much until they ended up in the same swamp. By then the poor woman was two strokes between alligators."

I nodded and sipped on the strong dark liquid. Portuguese and Cajun heritage made sure it could nail you to a wall. I chased it with the cool cantaloupe. "So she ended up cleaning houses, including Jacob's?"

"Off and on," said Pasquin. "I figure that didn't last. Woman is nosy as hell. Watches everything in these swamps. I mean," he shifted on the tree trunk, "how many ladies her age could navigate these woods and creeks and keep her residence a secret?"

I gazed into the thick swamp. Alice grew up here. Her father taught her boating. She'd know it all and would know how to survive the occasional snake bite, the overwhelming humidity, and the parasites that could eat through the skin. The woman seemed healthy as a horse outside her mind.

"Pasquin," I put the rest of my hot sausage aside. "Do you think

Alice still has those guns?"

The old man nodded. Gavi nodded, too. He licked his fingers of sausage grease. "She ain't parting with nothing her old man left her. Ain't much, but she's still got 'em, yessir!"

I pulled my cell phone from my pocket and dialed Tony Amado. "You'd best find Alice, Tony. She's got method and motive for killing men."

CHAPTER FIFTEEN

Tony said he wouldn't look for Alice. Said he didn't have enough men for a swamp search, and he was irritated with Pasquin for disappearing. "Get that old man to help you. He's got friends who might know where she is. When you find out, let me know!" He slammed down the phone. I smiled, knowing he would have deputies out looking in five minutes. I intended to get Pasquin's help, but I knew Tony wouldn't dare not look.

After calling Vernon and leaving a message on his phone that I would be home later in the day, I greeted a prodigal dog. Plato had been away from the camp the entire night. He tail was full of burrs, but he wagged his entire body when he saw me.

"Why in the world did I ever rescue you?" I scratched his ears and placed a pan of sausages in front of him. He took bites out of the spicy things and ran to the water's edge for a drink to cool the heat.

"Takes up with anybody, I'll bet," said Pasquin. He waved his hat at the dog as if he were going to hit him. Plato took that as a play offer and snapped at the frayed edges. He caught them between his teeth more than once. As though he knew the hat was an extension of the old man, he never ripped it apart.

"You ready to help me find a crazy swamp lady?" I asked Pasquin as he tired of playing with the dog, or Plato tired of playing with him. The dog moved down the river bank and found a sunny spot to plop down and rest.

"You thinking I'm going to galavant around the river right now?" Pasquin filled his coffee cup and sat hard on the tree trunk. "Won't help none. I done been asking about where that woman lives. Nobody knows for sure, mostly because they don't much care." He sipped loud enough to make Plato raise his head and stare at the man. "Might start caring when they hear about Jacob. First I hear she's got a cabin beyond Jacob's place. Then I hear again she's around here somewhere. She's got her own boat, but she can manage just about any kind of water vehicle. Her old daddy saw to that." Pasquin nodded toward a silent Gavi. "Best way to find where she lives is to follow her next time you see her."

I nodded. "Do you think she stole my canoe?"

"Could be. Don't know why, but could be." Pasquin bobbed his head up and down as though talking to some invisible being in front of him.

"She bashed a hole in it. Looks like she took an oar and just smashed it."

"Had some reason to do that," said Gavi. "Woman has a respect for boats. Doubt she'd do it unless she hated you or needed to take the canoe out of circulation."

"We found it near the place where Jacob's body was in the water." I remembered how the canoe had been dragged onto land and lay on its side with a smashed hole gaping upward. Had someone transported Jacob's body in it?

"Wouldn't take much for her to pull a canoe onto land and knock a hole in it," said Gavi. "She's always been a hefty woman."

I stood up. Hours of sitting on a tree trunk had numbed my backside and stiffened my joints. "Is Edwin taking me home?"

"My job," said Pasquin. "I'll drop you off. Maybe come back here."

"Be waiting," said Gavi and saluted with his coffee cup.

I thanked Gavi for the house tour. When I tried to coax Plato into the boat, he turned then headed off into the swamp.

"Dog thinks he's a bear," said Pasquin. He revved the motor and headed for the deep center of the creek. Before he got to full speed, he pulled out a rifle from its case and laid it across his knees. It wasn't for gators.

"You ever think somebody is going to take a pot shot at you from out there?" I pointed to the woods, so dense anyone could be there, ready to feed us to the fishies.

"Don't dwell on it," Pasquin said, "but I keep my eyes peeled."

"Pasquin," I looked closely at the weathered skin, the shock of white hair that blew in the breeze created by the movement of the boat. He never sped down the river, more like eased down it, staying in rhythm with its currents. "What do you think about when you sit around those campfires?"

He grinned, shoving up a thousand wrinkles into his face. "You getting philly-sophical, ma'am?"

"No, just wondering what goes on in that head of yours." I knew he wouldn't take it further without joking. Private thoughts stayed that way with Pasquin.

"Wonder sometimes why you don't marry that deputy and spring some river rats." He smiled. It was a nagging point with him.

"No river rats are going to spring off me," I said. "You're avoiding the question."

He nodded. The rest of the ride to my landing was spent in silence except for the occasional splash of some life form hitting the water in response to the vibration of the boat. A few early fishermen nodded and saluted as we moved down the river, but it was too early for most boat traffic.

"You'll let me know where you are?" I said as I held onto the landing post.

"Not unless I have to," said Pasquin. "Probably be back home soon anyway."

I stood on the landing, breathing in the still humid air that rose in a mist off the cold water. Pasquin's boat rounded the bend and vanished into the trees. "Just like Plato, you old water dog."

I needed rest. Being out nearly all night would take its toll later in the day, but at the moment I worried about a crazy old woman running the swamps with two rusty pistols. I walked to the end of my rutted road and retrieved the mail. Before I could make it back, a Volkswagen pulled up behind me.

"Harry?"

"Let's dive, Luanne. I feel brave right now and if I don't do it, I may never do it."

It wasn't the best thing to do without the rest of a night's sleep, but I had to agree. Harry needed to go down now. I moved into his car and let him drive me to the landing.

"Just give me a minute to get into a suit," I said. He had already begun pulling his tank from a space where the back seats should have been.

We sat on the edge of my landing, fins in the water, tanks on the back and face masks not yet lowered.

"Are you sure?" I asked.

"I'm sure."

"We'll go down here, then gradually make our way to the deep, cold water. You follow my lead. We'll go to the opening of the small cave out there below the cypress grove. You know, the one where we found the scuba cylinders stashed on the Twiggins case."

"It's narrow."

"We won't go inside. It's wide enough for you to push your upper body through if you hold your tank. Just do that. Pull off the tank, push your upper body, to the waist only, into the opening.

Maybe that kind of gradual entrance will give you courage. If you think you can't hold your tank and keep the mouthpiece in, just signal me and we'll stop."

Harry nodded. I nodded back and rolled into the water. He followed.

I went to the bottom in the few feet of water near the landing. Eel grass dotted the sand and I swam around it, brushing it with my hands and moving ever so slowly into deeper water. At one point, I felt the gush of a spring and a change in temperature. The bottom dropped abruptly and darkness greeted me. Harry still followed. His nod gave me the okay sign.

We moved into the dark water, its currents pushing around us. We could still see with surface light but soon we'd have to turn on the head lamps. Harry slowed when this kind of darkness overtook us. He seemed to be in a kind of sitting position in the water, suspended there with his lamp shining. I waited in front of him, thinking he would give the up sign. Instead, he nodded again.

I headed for the small cave. Its opening lay many feet below a heavy growth of cypress trees. The trees bordered a bank in the river bend. The water at these depths was cold and fresh, pushing out from the deep aquifer inside the cave. I reached the opening and shined a light all around the sides. Harry was behind me. He nodded again, signaling that he was sure there were no bombs planted. I moved aside and let him run his light around the opening. When he was satisfied, he nodded toward me and moved back. I pulled my tank straps off my shoulders and held them to one side so that the tank was even with my body. This would be the way one would have to go through a narrow opening. I swam into the cave up to my waist, carrying the tank with me. I hesitated, not wanting to look rushed and panicked. Then I backed out and replaced my tank on my back. I waved the go-ahead to Harry.

Harry hesitated but finally pulled at his straps. He seemed in a hurry. I took hold of his hands and motioned for him to slow down. He did and methodically removed the tank and held it at his side. He pushed his face to the cave entrance and stared inside. What went through his head at the moment, I couldn't know, but he suddenly shot into the opening then back out again. He nearly lost the tank with the rapid movement. I grabbed it and helped him replace it on his back. Both of us gave the up sign.

I headed for the landing, but Harry went straight up to the cypress grove. I followed and ended up several feet behind him. He had grabbed hold of a cypress knee and was clinging to it when I heard him yell, "Oh shit!"

The cypress trees formed a semi circular space of water. Somehow, Harry had cornered a moccasin in this space. The snakes are territorial and not incapable of striking on water. And this was one mad snake. Instead of crawling onto the cypress knees and moving away, it coiled on top of the water and struck out time after time. Harry was too far from it to be bitten, and a cornered snake was something he had faced before—before the bomb incident. Now, instead of backing out of the animal's territory, he held fast to the knee and cursed. His knuckles went white, and I was sure he was beginning to shake.

I swam to him and placed my hand under his chin. "Relax and come with me, Harry. The snake is far away. He can't touch you. Relax, it's the only way." It took several moments before he let go of the knee, but when he did, his body went limp. This was the best thing for me. I held him under his chin and swam back to the landing as I would have with a drowning man.

At the landing, he grabbed the ladder and held tight as I tried to remove both tanks. Hitching their straps onto the posts, I coaxed him into climbing out of the water. When both of us landed on the deck, he leaned into my chest and cried like a baby.

I'm not sure how long this moment lasted, but it came to a halt when I heard footsteps on the deck. Vernon stood above us; I sat with my back against a post and cradled Harry's head in my lap.

I shrugged and shook my head. Vernon leaned over and pulled up Harry, who still blubbered a bit. When he got to his feet, he staggered to the edge of the landing and sat down again, looking out to the river. He breathed hard but said nothing. Vernon pulled the tanks out of the water. His eyes darted to mine, and I finally saw the bitterness of jealousy peek through an accusatory glance. He said nothing.

We carried the tanks onto the porch and went back for Harry. He let us help him walk to the house. He trembled, a completely broken man. We wrapped him in a towel and sat him in a rocker on the front porch.

I went inside, a towel wrapped around my suit and sat on the edge of a chair.

"A snake freaked him out," I said.

"A snake?" Vernon's voice took on a sarcasm that I had never heard.

"A snake and diving, of course."

"Any reason you feel you have to take on the role of psychiatrist, Luanne?" Vernon's coldness shot through me like a fang.

"I'm sorry,. No reason. I never thought it would be this bad." My body trembled.

He didn't say anything else for nearly five minutes. When he did, he breathed hard and said, "I'm going to drive that man back to his place in the patrol car. You can follow in his car. Got that?"

I forced myself to nod and wondered if I could see to drive through the tears that had formed in my eyes. I felt both men slipping from me, one to the failure of courage, one to unfounded suspicion .

At Harry's place, Vernon paced the floor, then leaned against the wall several feet from both of us. I sat in a chair, my bathing suit dry now. Harry had calmed down and offered to pour everyone a scotch. Finally he drank one. He sat silent, as did I.

"The next time you get to campus, Luanne, find somebody in the psychology department to deal with this. And, Harry, if you can't dive, then for heaven's sake stay in your desk job." He headed for the door. "Coming Luanne, or do you see the need to stay the night?"

I followed him to the patrol car and sat in weepy silence while he headed back to my house.

"It's not anything like you seem to think it is," I said when I felt I could handle the lump in my throat.

"Not to you? But to him, what is it? Why does he keep running to you for help? And you seem to think you can give it."

"I can't. I know that now."

"It took something close to drowning to find that out?"

I nodded, unable to find an answer.

We stopped in front of my house. Vernon turned to me.

"Luanne, let the man find his own way. In all your eagerness to help, you're going to get him killed. And," he hesitated, "I don't particularly like seeing him groveling in your arms like that."

"Vernon…"

"I've never said I was jealous of your prior attachment to him, but surely you must know I don't exactly want the attachment to continue." He sat back in his seat. "We aren't married, and you are free to do as you please. But if you please to carry on with Harry MacAllister, then you won't carry on with me. Is that clear?"

I gulped and nodded.

We sat in silence until his radio came on and he was called back to the incident on the bay. I got out in silence and, with blurred eyes, watched his car back down the rutted road.

I slept for an hour at the most after my morning with Harry and Vernon. The silence of the house and its cocoon qualities couldn't comfort me. I fell into moping. I had to do something, to move and act to get the scenarios out of my head. Perhaps I could contact the department of psychiatry on campus and suggest a therapist for Harry. But Vernon's words burned in my brain, and I figured he was right. Harry had to find his own way.

I piled into the Honda, determined to go somewhere. While I was flying down the nearly deserted paved road, I thought about Georgie, the strange little man with all the information. Maybe I could drive into town and look at some of his maps.

The building where Georgie rented a room was on the edge of campus, a two-story craftsman-style house that was broken into small studio apartments. A student sat in a plastic chair on the front porch. He pointed the way to Georgie's room.

His door was the last on the second floor, down a shabby hallway that smelled of stale curry. I knocked. When no one answered, I wrote a note and planned on shoving it under the door. The ragged door mat had to be moved aside. That's when I saw the key. "Temptation!" I whispered and moved it into the keyhole.

The minute I opened the door, it hit an open closet door where a pair of military pants had been draped over the top. They fell to the cluttered floor, dropping contents before my feet. I stepped over them. Inside was a jumble of books, notebooks, smelly specimens, and clothes. The tiny utility kitchen needed a hosing down. I moved to a window and looked down into a backyard where more plastic chairs covered a broken patio. Georgie's bed was a tumble of clothes and sheets as though he slept underneath whatever was available. Returning to the fallen pants, I leaned over to retrieve the contents. I had no business doing this. Various pens and measurement tools greeted my fingers until I touched several small plastic bags. It took a quick whiff of the oregano-like smell to realize it was cannabis inside. "The damn kid is smoking, or worse, dealing!" I shoved them back into the pockets and tossed the pants over the closet door. I couldn't tell anyone about this. Not even Vernon. As an adjunct diver, paid by the sheriff's department, I was an officer of the law, and this was not a legal search.

I hurried from the room, replaced the key and dashed back to the front porch. Shoving the note into the hands of the student on the porch, I asked him to give it to Georgie when he returned. He nodded and stared at me—at least I could feel his eyes burning into my back—until the Honda turned the corner.

My swamp house had been renovated from a run-down family heritage place a few years back. The environment here has no mercy. Some dark spots appeared near the front door, where the screen kept out night bites; the paint was beginning to peel, losing its battle with humid air and molding leaves. The wooden rockers that sat on my porch, making like musical timers when I invited Pasquin for iced tea, needed painting. It was a task I suddenly longed to do, one that might pull me away from tracking down Alice and thinking about Georgie—and worst of all, thinking about losing Vernon. After my adventures of the day, I needed the cocoon that the swamp offered me. The phone rang.

"It's Barley Ben, Luanne." Vernon spoke on his cell phone. I could hear people yelling in the background. "Shot and dumped in the bay. Somebody pushed a heavy cooler into the drink with him.

He was on the bottom, his arms outstretched like he was playing catch and somebody threw a ball that was too heavy."

"Shot?" I started trembling. "Old men are getting scarce in this part of the country."

"In the head." Vernon turned his mouth away from the phone to speak to Tony.

"Like Jacob?"

"Like Jacob, and Otis Reynolds. Somebody likes aiming for the head."

Vernon spoke his news like nothing had changed, but then it was police information. I finally told him the news about seeing Pasquin and told him to keep it quiet. Holes in the head were not healthy for old men.

CHAPTER SIXTEEN

My immediate urge was to take off in the swamp and look for Alice. Guilt about the morning and thoughts of Tony and his deputies put me off that. He would have fits if he found me out there, searching alone, interfering with his troops. *And since when did I fear Tony?* Before I could answer myself, I heard the boat again, its distinctive high-pitched whine hanging for a second on the air as it sped down the river. The girls, I thought, had a death wish, one that would put them in the water with their sweet Tommy.

I hadn't seen Hanover's diver recently and wondered if he'd given up his bottom search. Asking Tony would give me a chance to find out what was happening with Alice and the Barley Ben scene. I dialed his cell phone.

"Far as we can tell, Hanover hasn't hired any other divers but that one. That kid is a goner, Luanne. Sucked out to sea or gulped down by a gator. Don't expect to see him again." Tony spoke from somewhere near where the Palmetto River emptied into the bay. "Right now, there's nobody on that scene. Too much happening here. Any more questions?"

"Are you searching for Alice?"

"Why should we?"

"She owns two guns, Tony." I shouted over the noise of a motor boat that echoed off his phone.

"You want to talk about this, Luanne. Get over here." Tony cut me off. Vernon often told me this was his way of prodding a person into action, of doing what he wanted without a direct order. The idea of Alice's two guns intrigued him enough to want to know more. At least that's what I wanted to think.

I grabbed my high boots and headed out the door. If Tony wanted the information firsthand, he'd get it that way.

Just in case, I loaded the scuba gear into my Honda. As I readied to leave, I heard the motor boat come screeching back my way. I ran to the landing in time to see Roxanna and Patsy in the front seats. Both were laughing; Roxanna swerved the boat in S shapes on the water, creating huge wakes that sloshed against the banks.

I yelled "slow down" again, but neither even knew I was standing there. They rounded the bend and the engine whine faded away.

I would have preferred to go by boat but my transport in the form of Pasquin was off hiding at Portu Landing. Instead, I bumped along the rutted road to the paved road then onto the highway. When I pulled into the bay site, a light rain was falling.

"You planning on diving?" asked Loman as he met me at the car. "We already pulled the body out."

"No. I'm planning on talking to Tony. That's kind of like diving with no air," I said and pointed to the spot where Tony was talking to Marshall Long. At their feet lay a bulge on a tarp. "Barley Ben?"

Loman nodded. "And this time it wasn't booze that hurled him into the bay."

Umbrellas popped open as the rain came down harder. Someone tossed another plastic tarp over the body. When Marshall stooped over one end, he lifted off the tarp. Another tech stood over his head with an umbrella, but his protruding bottom got a drenching.

I joined Tony who stood under a tree. His own umbrella, a black one, matched his perfect hair. Not a drop showed on his shirt or pants.

"Okay, what is this about Alice?"

I told him the story that Gavi had related about her WW2 guns and shooting at the young man who insulted her advances.

"So you think she may have opened up on these three old men?" Tony looked out over the bay, his head nodding slightly.

"I don't know. It's just that she was around the swamps, where both of them lived. And she was there that day we found Jacob. She had this little stone memorial she danced around. Sounds crazy, but then maybe she is."

"She is," nodded Tony. "But is she homicidal?"

"You planning on finding her?"

Tony's jaw clenched; his olive skin reddened a bit. "Probably. But we got this problem right now." He nodded toward Marshall who nearly tumbled over the body as he leaned to check something. Two techs grabbed his arms and hauled his bulk to a standing position.

"Any news on the Hanover kid?" I knew the answer before Tony stared at me and shook his head.

"His old man seems to have gone off on a business trip. Left his pretty wife to tend to the river cabin and pay the diver. He's still at it, you know. Still poking around the banks where the boat hit the manatee." Tony nodded back in the direction of the river. "Funny that his wife hasn't gone back to her fancy house in town."

"Those girls, Roxanna and Patsy," I said, "I see them racing up and down the river in a speed boat, having a ball."

Tony stayed silent. He wouldn't look at me, but the jaw gave away his thinking process. "Really?" he finally said, and walked away from me toward Marshall Long. He stood there, in the rain, then turned and headed for his car.

Whether or not my usefulness had run its course with Tony

wasn't going to become evident. Looking for Alice in a monsoon seemed a whole lot more satisfying at the moment. She had shown up when we found Jacob. Would she be around here now? She even showed up in the woods near where we were searching for Tommy Hanover and ended up finding Otis, or what was left of him.

I backed the Honda away from the herd of patrol cars and scene wagons and headed down a gravel road that led to a small landing at the end of a private dock. Just around the river bend the Hanover house was hidden in its grove of trees. I sat and waited for the torrents to ease up then opened the umbrella and eased onto the muddy side of the road. The ditch, deep and full of reeds, was slowly becoming a little lake from the rain and the overflowing river. If I stepped too close, the mud would give way and I'd tumble into the narrow stream. Across the ditch, the wooden deck of the land-ing was taking a pounding. The two speed boats tied up there bounced and protested their ropes. Across the river, two young fishermen struggled to pull their small boat into a slip. They must have been caught out on the bay as their clothes were drenched. They waved to me once they had tied up and scrambled onto the landing.

Where to begin to look for Alice? I tried to put myself in the mad woman's place. She lived in the swamp, or at least had a place to stay here, because she was around so often. She had once tucked herself into an abandoned motel cottage. She cleaned Jacob's house. She knew the area around Nettleson's trailer. "Hell, she knew the place where Jacob was found and she grew up way over on Portu Landing." This wasn't going to be easy.

I pulled out my cell phone and dialed Georgie Emment's num-ber. Sitting inside the Honda, I shut out the pounding rain. "Did you get the note I left with a house mate of yours? Does the uni-versity know where these abandoned trailers, and maybe other

abodes, exist in the swamps out here, and if so, are they on a map?"
I left the message and orders to call me back. The rain was blinding
and nearly deafening as sheets hit the windshield. Through it all, I
glimpsed dim lights behind me. Not long after, a figure in a black
rain slick tapped on my window.

"Ma'am, this is private property." A deputy peered in at me
through the small space I gave him. "Oh, Ms. Fogarty, sorry. I got
a call about somebody's car, and…"

"It's okay. I'm leaving as soon as the rain lets up. Just checking
out something." I turned to face the man. His rain slick had edged
up in the back. Rain drops hit the back of his starched shirt and
soaked through to the bullet proof vest. "You'd best get out of it
yourself."

He nodded and headed behind my car. I remembered what I
came for and quickly rolled down the window. Rain nearly flooded
the seat. "Deputy!"

Like a black swamp ghost, the man reappeared at my window.
"Ma'am?"

"Do you know Crazy Alice Calder?" I had to yell over the pounding water.

"Of course. The woman—or calls about her—get me out of
bed in the middle of the night at least twice a year."

"Any idea where she lives?"

"Not exactly. She had a little cabin somewhere near Scrapper
Creek the last I heard. She lives wherever she wants. Even in people's
garages at times." He made an attempt to laugh, but a splash of rain
hit him in the side of the face.

"Thanks!" I said and rolled up the window. He disappeared into
the wet. Shortly afterwards, I saw the headlights fade behind me.

When the rain had settled into a drizzle, I moved the Honda
onto the paved road and headed for Palmetto Springs. I had seen a

canoe shop there and hoped for a nice rental. I wasn't disappointed.

The place was housed in something that could have been an old quonset hut. The owner had placed special shelves on the walls to hold up various canoes, some new aluminum, some old and expensive wood. On the wall behind the cash register hung an ancient canoe. I skirted the room until I came to the section under a FOR RENT sign. Several had SEYMOUR printed on their sides. I picked one nearly the same as the one I lost and paid the man. As his son climbed to its location on the wall, the door opened and in walked Tommy Hanover's father. He was dressed in khaki pants and a sports coat and wore boat shoes. He asked the owner if anything new had come up about his son.

"Anyway," said Hanover in a louder voice, "I've got to get on with making a living. Two wives to support ain't cheap." He made an attempt at a sarcastic laugh. "I'm showing some land. You got the key to my boat?"

The owner's son carried the light canoe in his arms and nodded for me to show the way to my car.

"Wasn't that Mr. Hanover in there?" I was sure the kid wouldn't know I had been working on the case.

"Yeah. His son drowned, so they say."

"I heard. I'm surprised you rent him boats. I would have thought he'd be rich enough to own his."

"He owns several. Keeps them in various places. We rent him space here, and he drops by for it every now and then. Nice thirty-footer."

I helped the boy place the canoe on top of the Honda and thanked him. As I drove away, I saw Hanover back his car up to a boat shed.

"Tony said the man had to go out of town. Short trip," I said as I pulled onto the highway.

I'd start at Scrapper Creek and move into the woods behind Jacob's house. Alice, if she was living back there, may have moved on as the cops would have been all over Jacob's place after his murder. My first stop would be Nettleson's trailer.

Sam Nettleson found out just what he was living in when the rainstorm hit. By the time I paddled a rented canoe to the end of Scrapper Creek and stashed it under the bushes that grew on the banks, the rain had settled to a drizzle. It had completely stopped when I tromped through the muddy woods and stood before a flooded test station.

Nettleson was tossing down some pieces of wood in the back when I surprised him.

"Love your roofing," I said and pointed to the black tarp that had been spread across half the rusty trailer.

"Damn rain," he said. "Nearly made a bath tub out of the place." He pressed the wood with one foot, barefoot this time. From the looks of the dirt, he had been walking around in water and mud for a while. "I'm trying to make a walkway to the table."

Nettleson's table of samples was bare now. Standing water rested on top, and the whole thing leaned because one leg had sunk into a mud puddle.

"You need some help?"

He glanced at me and shook his head. "No!" He put up his hand as though to ward off the evil eye. "I can't afford to have a stranger touching the experiments and samples." He turned and slammed the flimsy door behind him.

"At least let me help you shore up the table." I followed him across the boards that sank in the oozing mud. He didn't object when I took one corner and helped him lift one end and move the table to more solid earth.

"Thanks. I'll be okay now." He sat on the edge of the table and breathed a heavy sigh.

"Tired?"

"Been on the roof and hauling in supplies out of the rain. Had to do it pretty damn quick, too." His eyes darted toward me and back again.

"Have you seen Alice out here lately?"

My question caught him, and he stared at me for a moment. "No, and I don't want to see her. Why?"

"Just looking for her. She's needed at the sheriff's department."

"What'd she do, steal somebody's husband?" He laughed.

"Not sure she did anything. Did you hear about Jacob?"

"Yeah. Poor old sot. Had to admire the man living out here all the time." Nettleson fanned his hand in the air. It was almost a gesture of disdain toward the swamp around him. "Don't think I'd stay here without a damn good reason."

"And testing water samples is your reason?" I stared at the man, waiting for his lie.

He nodded. "Fun job, lady." He didn't look at me. I wondered just how long he planned to keep up the facade of being a university student.

"You use that holding pond back there where we ran into you the other day?"

Nettleson looked up quickly, then away. "It's a good way to get supplies in here from the other side," he said. "Fellow brings them in on a truck."

"Just for you? Seems a lot of bother when you could get someone to come down Scrapper Creek, or even go after them yourself."

He glanced my way again. "No," he shook his head. "Some of

the stuff is too delicate and cumbersome. I like it better by truck."

I didn't say anything, but I thought, "I'll bet you do. Trucks to haul out hydrilla that will become poison pills disguised as vitamins."

"If you see Alice, give me a call." I handed him a card with my cell phone number on it. I left him sitting on his table and walked back around front. The door to the trailer was slightly ajar. I stopped and pushed it a bit more. Inside was packed with large bundles that looked like neatly bundled laundry at first. Most likely dried hydrilla, I thought. That pungent odor hit me again, and I wondered how Nettleson could sleep all night in a place like that.

I pushed through the wet scrub, my boots making deep tracks in the fresh mud. The swamp was coming to life again. Birds sang in the after-rain. Several yards into the woods on the way to Jacob's house, I turned back. Sam Nettleson stood in front of his trailer, watching me move into the forest.

CHAPTER SEVENTEEN

Finding Jacob's house was easy. I just followed the muddy trail. The rain had gouged it out to the point of being a rut that ran right to the front door. And Jacob would have been astounded if he could have seen the place. Yellow tape that had a day ago formed an X across the door, hung wet and loose. Other tape that must have surrounded the house during the search lay half-buried in mud.

I skirted the place, looking into the tiny windows. At one point I could see the black dust of the fingerprint crew. The place had been gone over and nothing found to indicate who blew the man's brains out.

There were no footprints left. Even those of the scene techs and deputies had been washed away by the heavy rain. But the rain had left another rutted path into the woods behind the house. It lasted only a few yards until the scrub took over, but it was a starting place. I followed it and nearly ran into the side of another rusted trailer, the rounded kind that would hold, maybe, two campers. It sat on crumbling cement blocks. The one small window on this side sat high in the arc, its slats closed tight as though they hadn't been opened for years. There was a window on the small door at one end, but it was boarded shut. Three cement blocks served as steps. They were clean, but that could have been from the rain. The rest of the trailer was nearly covered in kudzu vines, the stuff that screamed "abandoned house." It grew to the rounded top, skirting around the window and draping over the door. "Most likely a live oak snake lives inside," I whispered to the elements.

I had to push aside some scrub to make my way around the rusted abode. The kudzu wasn't so thick on the other side, but it was there, waiting to take off in a spurt of growth that would strangle the thin walls in a season. A closed slatted window graced this side, too. Fighting the impulse to go barging inside, I stood looking at the trailer and wondered how it ever got pulled into this part of the forest. Something cracked behind me.

I turned. When the sound didn't repeat itself, I had visions of a watcher in the woods. Rather than hide from an unknown fiend, which could be baby deer, I faced the sound and walked to the edge of the trees. Feet pounded on the forest floor. Not the four hooves of a deer but the two shod ones of a human. A glimpse of something like ghost plasma shot ahead of me. Gray hair came to mind, and I figured Alice had been watching. I ran after her sound. Scrub and tree bark scratched my hands and arms, even one cheek. I darted and dodged but finally gave up when I came to a depression in a tiny clearing. I found no prints. *How does that woman know where to run?* Edging around the muddy depression, which was most likely a sinkhole that I wanted to avoid, I moved to the other side. The trees and bushes were just as thick here, with no sign of anyone making an entrance back into the woods.

Standing still and quiet, I thought I heard splashing water. It was faint, almost like an anhinga bird ducking under for a water snail. A few yards through the trees, and I reached a circular sinkhole. It would be just as deep at the shoreline as it was in the middle. Deep meant no bottom at all.

I stood at the edge, gazing into the black water then around at the thickness of the forest. There were no sounds of birds, reptiles, or insects. In a flash, there was the sound of a gunshot, one that flew over my head and thudded into a tree trunk behind me. I turned and looked for a way into the woods, but another shot rang out, its hot wind striking palmetto bushes a few yards away. I took the way I knew best. I dove into the water.

Holding my breath, I headed downward and threw my arms around a tree branch that had lodged itself on one wall of the sink. The darkness of the water was broken only when I looked upward where the sun barely illumined the surface. In an instant, I heard the slow motion thud of a bullet hitting water and passing through until the denser medium slowed it to a halt. I pulled on the tree branch and eased further down the sinkhole. My body backed into the dirt walls and tried to blend in. My lungs began to burn.

After what seemed an eternity, no more shots rang out. I used the sink walls to float slowly upward, gasping for air as soon as I reached the surface. From my niche in the shadows of the bank, I looked around the rim, expecting to see a naked gray-haired woman pointing a World War II pistol at me. No one appeared, and nothing happened. I held myself in the cold water until I realized the forest fauna were communicating again. Climbing out proved difficult. The sides of the banks were steep and made of crumbly dirt. I left clear foot and body prints of my struggle.

Sticking to the woods, I walked quietly back to the clearing, then again found the rusted trailer. It could wait. My clothes were wet, and I couldn't be sure the gunner wasn't following me. My fear turned to anger and I needed to get to Amado and his deputies. I made a quick visual check to make sure no one waited in the shade of the kudzu, then scurried past the trailer. Ten steps into the forest, I stopped.

Turning back, I looked again at one side of the trailer. The slatted window. It was open, and it hadn't been earlier. Easing to the cement steps, I could see the muddy prints of bare feet. It had to be Alice.

I picked up one of the loose cement blocks from the front steps and placed it underneath the open slats of the window. Standing on tiptoe, I was able to glance downward into a dark and crowded room. My eyes adjusted to the dimness to see at first what seemed like an animal that breathed slowly. As my eyes focused, I realized the animal was flesh colored, a flat surface with something in the middle. A ring! A navel ring, attached to the middle, rose and fell with the sleeping breaths of a human being.

I waited on the side for a sound of someone inside, but nothing happened. The forest animals kept up their monotony. There was no disturbance of nature.

Replacing the cement step, I eased open the door. It made no sound. Someone had oiled the hinges. I dreaded the tilt that surely would happen the minute I put my weight inside. It happened, but no one darted to defend the territory. A curtain had been hung a few steps from the front door, almost like a mosquito net or privacy device. I pushed it aside. There, amid a clutter of towels, pans, and a first aid kit from the Ocean Pine Motel, lay a form on a cot. It was a young adult male, nude, a bit bruised about the shoulders and head, one leg strapped between two boards below the knee, his arms tied to the bed springs at the wrists—and in a deep sleep. But it was the navel ring that identified him to me. "Tommy Hanover," I whispered. "No wonder we never found you in the water."

I made an attempt to shake the boy, but he didn't respond. He seemed drugged, and I had no way to transport him right now. Before heading to my canoe, I glimpsed the little rock monument at the end of the bed. Fresh yellow flowers had been placed in the crevices.

A light drizzle started as I pushed back through the scrub, finally arriving at Jacob's house. I would have tried the cell phone here, but I had lost it in the pit of a sinkhole. It would be on its way to the Gulf by now, passing through a maze of deep cave tunnels. The drizzle turned to rain, and I plastered myself against the house, hoping the slight edge of the roof would keep me dry. It made no sense. I was all ready wet. I stepped into the rain and followed the rivulets back to the edge of Nettleson's place. Perhaps I should have stopped and asked for his help, but I saw no sign of him, and who trusted a poison pill maker, anyway? I pushed on, longing for my canoe and oars.

They weren't there. I had carefully tucked the canoe under bushes and anchored it there with the oars. "Not again!" I cried. And this time, I had no way of calling anyone to come for me.

Rain dripped across my face. I thought of walking back along the creek and maybe finding someone to get a ride with, but decided to seek out Nettleson, instead.

I shoved back into the forest, sloshing through mud and broken down scrub brush. Nettleson's trailer stood there with rain pounding the black tarp and muddy water rushing around the front steps. It looked a lot like the one deeper in the woods, the one with Tommy Hanover. I shuddered.

No on answered my knock. I shoved at the door but it was locked tight and felt as though something barred it from the inside. Moving around back required balancing myself with one hand against the side of the trailer. The muddy water was quickly turning to a flood.

The back door was latched but a good jerk and I had it open. I stood inside a darkened space. Instead of opening into a kitchenette or even a sitting area, it appeared to be a foyer, albeit a tiny one. Nettleson, or someone, had built three walls around a tiny space. In one wall there was door, locked tight with a dead bolt. The flimsy little trailer was misleading. The place was locked up like a safe.

I stood inside the foyer and let the wet drip off me. When

Nettleson returned, he'd see the break-in, but he could rest assured no one got into the inner sanctum of his test site. Even in this little hole, I could smell the pungent odor. It reminded me of oregano, and then it hit me. Of course! Nettleson comforted himself in this wicked swamp with a little pot smoking.

When the rain let up, I headed past Jacob's and the holding pond where Nettleson harvested the hydrilla. My luck took hold again. A pickup truck sat at the water's edge. Its driver leaned against the back as though waiting for someone.

"You don't happen to have a cell phone on you?" I asked as I waved across the pond.

The man, startled at seeing a woman in the swamp, took out the phone and waved it in the air.

"My boat got stolen. Can you call a number for me?"

The man looked about as though hoping no one could see us. He finally called back, "What's the number?"

He dialed, then jerked the phone from his ear, placed his hand over the mouthpiece, and yelled, "Lady! That's the sheriff's office."

"I know. Tell them Luanne Fogarty is stuck in the woods and will meet them at the end of Scrapper Creek. And to hurry!"

The man turned back and gave the message. I thanked him, watched him wave, and jump into the cab and drive away, his tires whining in the mud.

"That's right. Get out before the cops arrive." I smiled and headed back to Scrapper Creek.

"Woman, you got to stop doing this," said Loman. He had again been sent to fetch me. "I been rescuing people all day. That diver Hanover hired, had himself a heart attack right on shore this morning, and now you." A uniform deputy said nothing but smiled at the man's agitation.

"You've got to get the cops into these woods," I said. "I was nearly killed. And there's another rescue waiting for you in a trailer back there."

CHAPTER EIGHTEEN

Moving a force of deputies, their posses, crime scene techs, and the rescue squad into a dense swamp after a rainstorm, with old man Hanover right on their tail when he heard his son was alive, sent the forces of nature into a panic. Patrol boats lined up, military style, from the river to the end of Scrapper Creek. Yellow tape, tacked to trees, marked the way into the swamp, past Nettleson's trailer and Jacob's cabin, all the way to the little trailer where Tommy lay strapped in all his injuries. Beyond that, deputies searched for bullets in trees and poured plaster into muddy footprints.

"We've got a search party, such as it is, out looking for Alice," said Tony. His eyes darted away from me at intervals.

"What the hell was she doing with my son?" An enraged Hanover, still dressed in his sports coat, trudged through the mud to speak to Tony. Tony, his jaw working steadily, flashed a look of momentary abject pain.

"We'll find that out when we find her," said Tony.

A few yards away, paramedics lifted Tommy onto a stretcher and carried him into the woods. The plan was to have an ambulance waiting at the road that led to the holding pond. In fact, activity at the holding pond assured that no hydrilla would be collected today.

"My son is still out of it," moaned Hanover, his arms waving through the air. "How did she get him here?" He wandered off behind the stretcher.

A deputy in a white coat came out of the trailer, his gloved hand holding a paper bag. "Got sleeping pill bottles," he said as he approached Tony, "and each one is prescribed for a different person."

"She stole them, I'll bet," I said, remembering Alice's antics at the Ocean Pine Motel. "She got her man and the only way to keep him was to drug him."

Another tech came from the trailer with a large cardboard box. "Found four of these boxes with vials in them. Think somebody was experimenting with drugs or something?" He held the box so Tony and I could peek inside.

"Those are Nettleson's experiment supplies," I said. "Just like the one we found in the water at the end of the creek. I'll bet Alice has been stealing them. He said somebody had stolen things from his trailer."

People glanced around nervously, half-looking for a swamp woman who could sneak naked through the scrub and wield guns at the same time. And, I figured, get rid of a canoe.

"Anybody diving in Scrapper Creek?" I asked.

"Vernon's up there now." Tony turned his attention to another white-coated man.

"Got somebody digging the bullet out of a tree," he said. "You say we're to look for old guns, .38 revolvers from World War II?"

Tony nodded and went to the trailer to check on the search team.

"Any chance of a canine unit?" I called after him.

"Maybe. Lots of water around here. May not work with the dogs." Tony answered his cell phone. "You want to get up to Scrapper Creek, Luanne. They found your canoe. Want you to identify it."

I headed back through the swamp that now had a widened trail from Scrapper Creek to the little trailer. When all this ended, it would take maybe a day for the growth to take over again, make it look as though no one was ever there. The thought gave me pause. Most of us would hike down a tried and true path, one that wouldn't hide reptiles and stinging ivy. But, if you wanted to hide your tracks, you might take a different way each time, tread on virgin grass and leave no marks. That would be dangerous in a swamp, but someone like Alice might do it. She seemed to have an animal nature about her.

Vernon sat on the far bank of Scrapper Creek, resting from having pulled up the rented canoe. The boat lay on one side, exposing a long slash cut right down the bottom. "Had to be with an ax," said Vernon. "I checked the bank and you can see in the dirt there where the blade gouged out some chunks. The oar is chopped into kindling, too." He pointed to some scraps of wood higher on the bank. "You're gonna owe the rental company."

"These creeks do seem to be canoe graveyards," I said.

"More like where canoes go to be murdered," he added. "The action on this canoe looks like anger. Those others we saw in Grandpa's Creek, I wonder now if they weren't deliberately sunk."

"Alice?"

We stood on opposite sides of the bank, imagining a wild woman, old but strong, with her long gray hair flying about her as she raised an ax and chopped at the boats. Was it because she saw them as infringing on her territory? Learning her secrets?

"She's going to be one rare psychiatric case when they find her," said Vernon.

He edged into the water and swam to my side. I helped him with his fins and tank.

"I heard that Hanover's diver had a heart attack."

Vernon grunted. "That's a strange one, too. Somebody, a woman's voice, called 911 to report a diver in trouble along the entry to Grandpa's Creek. When the emergency techs got there, he was lying flat on his back on shore. His tank, fins, and mask were set neatly in a row a few feet away. And his suit was unzipped to the waist."

"Maybe he did that before the attack."

"Would you?" Vernon leaned against a tree and slapped at a horsefly. "I mean think about it. You're tanking up, or maybe already in the water, and you get chest pains. You stagger on shore— pull off the equipment, arrange it in precise spots, unzip your suit and go lie down on the bank over there."

"Sure, why not? And I'd ask the first mermaid to call the doctor."

"We need to question Hanover about the man, but he's out there right now." Vernon ignored my attempt at humor and waved toward the swamp.

"They took Tommy away. You can probably find his father at the hospital."

Vernon and I left the wrecked canoe with the scene techs and caught a ride with a patrol boat back to the Palmetto River location. Sheriff presence was heavy here. They had blocked off all roads, water as well as dirt and pavement, to the area. Fishermen forgot to curse at losing a day in their boats and sat open-mouthed at the news of Tommy Hanover's rescue. Among the visitors trying to move into the area was the media, television and newspaper. We dodged the cameras and ended up in my Honda. Before we could start out, a familiar bundle of a man came running into the area, a uniformed deputy of rather wide girth chasing after him.

"It's Georgie," I said and rolled down the window.

"Can you get these people off my tail?" He panted from the run as he grasped the window. "I've been trying and trying to call your cell phone."

"It's somewhere in the abyss of a sinkhole," I said. "Lost it when I dodged bullets."

"What?" Georgie inhaled and stepped backward. He landed in the arms of the deputy.

"Okay, son, what's going on here?" The man held him just above his elbows.

I reassured the deputy he was okay and invited Georgie to sit inside the car.

"You've got something?"

Vernon and I turned to watch the man squeeze his odd little frame into the small back seat.

"I been watching those guys bring in the hydrilla. They got a barn over by the highway where they store it before they cart it off to be dried and crushed into pills. But," he hesitated, his eyes wide and unblinking, "when I got inside that place, I figured out why they're making so much money off the stuff."

The car was silent. The three of us dripped in sweat from the humidity. Vernon finally said, "Are you planning on telling us?"

"Yeah! Well, see, they don't have too many guys staying around this place, so I got into a back door. Kind of reminds you of an old tobacco barn. Got lots of grass in piles, some wet, some dry. I start looking at it and move toward the front of the barn where they got double doors, locked, of course. And guess what I found in between loads of hydrilla?"

More silence.

"Grass."

"You told us that, Georgie. Hydrilla grass all over the place." Vernon was getting restless.

"No, *grass*, the puff-puff kind." He made a motion with his fingers as though he were smoking a cigarette.

"Marijuana?" Vernon reached for his phone.

"That's it!" Georgie grinned and clapped his hands once like we'd won a quiz.

"Nettleson's trailer," I said, facing Vernon. "He has this secure foyer in the back. Couldn't be water tests or hydrilla he wanted to lock up tight."

"We don't have proof it's Nettleson doing this. Tony won't be able to get a search warrant unless we have more evidence." He turned to Georgie who wiggled like a kid in the back seat. "You rocking this car for a reason?"

"I got an idea. See," Georgie inhaled and began his presentation as though the audience would walk out any minute, "north of Scrapper Creek, there's some open land here and there, land without marshes. I've been looking on some maps, and I can show you." He stared at both of us, his head nodding in his own approval.

"Okay, where?"

He told me where to drive. We ended up at a make-shift hut on the edge of the county.

"Been working at this site for a while. Cave system extends through three counties. Did you know that?"

"Georgie," I said, "these maps aren't inside the caves are they?"

He laughed. "Of course not! They're in the hut. We use them to plot where we are and what bacteria grows where." He laughed again and hauled himself out of the back seat. Before entering the hut, he hiked up his belted pants.

"You believe this?" said Vernon.

"He's got a genius brain, Vernon. It works in mysterious ways." I pushed myself into the afternoon heat and followed Georgia inside the boxy hut.

"Now here we are," he said as he opened up a large map. "Here's the bridge at Palmetto River and Scrapper Creek is right here." He poked a chubby finger at the paper. It was easy to notice the dirt under his nails. "And if you go north, you'll see less sinkholes, marshes, and other low-lying wet places. It all turns into flat and fertile land, but only in spots."

"And that's good, is it?" I gazed at the man.

"If you want to hide a growth, that's real good." Georgie tried to do a Southern drawl imitation. "You'd plant amongst the pines and oaks and other trees. Anybody walking through, might not realize what the plants are. Of course, some might realize what they are and take advantage."

"And you think it's Nettleson?" Vernon looked first at Georgie, then at me.

"Well," I added, "he is helping to gather the hydrilla. At least that's what Georgie says."

"But not alone," said Georgie. "He's got people to pull it out of the water and cart it off. Same people most likely harvest the weed and cart it off, too."

"No wonder that guy at the pond high-tailed it when I asked him to call the sheriff. And I thought it was hydrilla."

Georgie looked perplexed for a moment. "You gotta remember what I told you. Harvesting hydrilla and selling the pills is not government regulated. It's not a crime."

"And now we're supposed to search this area," Vernon pointed to spot north of Scrapper Creek, "for marijuana plants and signs of this Nettleson?"

"Any possibility Alice is in on this?" I envisioned the old lady dancing in the nude and smoking a reefer as she sang her chant of knowing what to do.

"Alice?" Georgie shrugged. "I only know Nettleson, but can we get going?"

"Who owns the land?" Vernon asked.

Georgie's face fell. He shook his head, knowing this would put a stop to any search until we either had owner permission or we found it was open government land. He'd been through this too many times on university research to think we could just walk out there and start snooping.

While Georgie spilled out ways he thought we could get on the property through his work, Vernon answered a cell call.

"It's Tony," he said, "he wants us to meet at Mama's Table tonight. The whole team will stay in the woods all night if they don't find Alice. He thinks she's too dangerous to run loose."

Georgie looked around eagerly. "Can I go and explain why we need to search here?" He poked his finger on the map.

Vernon shrugged. "You'll have to go, I guess. You've found marijuana and even if it has nothing to do with this case, it's a crime." He stopped and stared at Georgie's silly grin and nearly laughed himself. "And bring that map."

Mama's Table was always at the ready for the sheriff's department. It had been the unofficial center of many a crime discussion. Tonight was a little closer to the official as Tony didn't want to haul everyone back to Tallahassee. There we sat at three pushed-together tables in the rear of the small cafe. A few fishermen came to eat up near the front, but Mama, her wide hips and newly bleached hair denoting her as boss, kept them away from our table.

Loman and Tony sat at one end, Vernon and I at the other. Marshall Long took up the center, his thighs hanging over the plastic seat of the chair. Georgie took a seat near him. As one scientist to another, he had an admiration that bordered on rock fan. Two seats were vacant.

"Somebody else coming?" I asked.

Tony gave a half smile. "I got the river brigade out and found someone we need to talk to." Before he finished, Gavi and Pasquin walked into the cafe.

Gavi's dark eyes gave no sign that he felt anything about his beckoning. His tall old body sat down and picked up a menu. Pasquin, on the other hand, pulled off his straw hat and walloped me with it.

"You're back in civilization!" I said as I dodged the tattered hat.

"Civilization? Okay, maybe the food." He picked up the menu; the two men had had about enough of their own cooking. "Sheriff's paying, right?" He didn't wait for Tony to answer, just went ahead and ordered a big plate of fried oysters.

When everyone had ordered, Tony placed both hands on the table and began as though he were a preacher on circuit.

"Marshall here tells us we got similar bullet holes in two heads."

"Three," said Marshall as he tore off a tail shell from a boiled shrimp. "Otis from a year back has the same kind of hole."

"Okay," Tony said, breathing out once in disgust at having been interrupted so soon into his session. "Three men, three similar bullet holes in the head. And we've got a kid who's been held in a trailer for several days..."

"How do you know he's been in that same place all those days?" I asked. I pulled apart a fried grouper finger and dipped it in tartar sauce.

"Well, we don't for sure, but it looks like he was being fed on soup for quite some time. And drugged. I've got deputies checking out former guests of the Ocean Pine to see if any of their sleeping pills were stolen. And, ballistics hasn't finished but the bullets they pulled from the trees are .38s, consistent with what could have been fired from old World War II pistols. Like those Alice owns." He looked at me quickly then glanced away. "And there's the rock and flower memorial you found."

"All adds up to Crazy Alice," I said.

"No," said Pasquin, "not the shooting part. Now, maybe she'll shoot at a man. She's shot at one before in front of people. But why at a woman?"

"Not like her to hide, either," said Gavi. He swirled melted cheese around in his grits. "She always did her crazy stunts right out in the open."

Tony tossed up his hands, "Maybe she thought Luanne was stealing her man." He turned his attention to the trout fillet on his plate.

"Can I tell now?" Georgie spoke up, his mouth full of hush puppy.

"Tell what?" Tony put down his fork. Pulling apart fried fish with his fingers wasn't his talent.

Georgie pulled out the map and spread it over the table. Mama found this curious and most likely a bit insulting to her cooking. She came and looked over Georgie's shoulder. He began with the hydrilla barn and the marijuana find, and ended with his theory that someone could be growing it north of Scrapper Creek. "And Sam Nettleson might know what's going on," he ended with a proud grin.

"Uh-huh," said Marshall. "Can we move the map now? My oysters are getting cold."

"Marijuana?" said Tony. He ate for a few minutes, then looked at Loman. "Get search warrants for the barn and the property north of the creek."

Loman's sad eyes took on a weeping bloodhound effect. He stared at Tony, who didn't look back at him. Giving up, he motioned for Mama to box his dinner.

"Now what you going to do about poor old Alice?" asked Pasquin. "Lady don't need to be running around the woods with two pistols."

"I'd suggest we check out the Ocean Pine Motel again. She had a first aid kit from there." I noticed Calvin working the front tables. "Maybe he can help."

Calvin's forehead dripped with sweat from bussing tables and cleaning the kitchen. No doubt he had worked all day at his family's restaurant and motel before coming here. "She hasn't actually worked for us for some time," he said when asked about Alice.

"But she knows the rooms," I said. "Could she break into them and steal stuff from guests? Maybe even live there?"

"No. We clean those rooms even when there are no guests. Mildew, you know. If someone had tried to live there, we'd know. Now, I suppose she could break in, even get in with a key if she made a copy. We never changed the locks after we let her go."

"Calvin, is there any place where, say, a homeless person could get in and live without you knowing, some place other than the old cabins in the back?"

Calvin leaned against the table and rubbed his thumbs up and down the straps on his apron. "Way back in the woods and down closer to the water, there are some old rusted trailers. Used to be part of rentals years back. Nobody ever goes back there now. And there used to be a fish cleaning shed back there when boats ran that part of the bay." He stood up and smiled. "But I sure wouldn't want to go snooping in those old scraps. Snakes and bugs probably set up housekeeping in them by now."

"And boats," I said, "does anyone keep boats on that part of the bay these days?"

"Nobody that I know of. There used to be a boat house and landing down there but I heard they got wiped out by the last hurricane. Whole area is overgrown in palmetto. A boater couldn't see a landing even if one still existed."

"All the better place to hide one's own," I said.

CHAPTER NINETEEN

Pasquin took Gavi home with him. The two rode in his boat and would stay there with shotguns by their beds for the night. I had visions of the octogenarians hearing each other in the dark and blasting away. Pasquin said most likely they'd never hear an intruder over their own snoring. "Well, check under the beds when you get there. Maybe Alice likes your house the best."

None of us would have been surprised to find Alice holed up in someone's vacant house, or maybe in a barn. That's when the idea hit me. What if Alice had found the hydrilla barn and moved in there. She wouldn't have been a welcome guest, especially if she realized pot was being harvested and stored there along with her sandals and rock memorials.

The night took on a surreal quality. Georgie was to go out with us the next day to point the way to the "might be" fields north of Scrapper Creek and to lead us to the barn. Instead of traveling all the way into town to his shabby apartment near the campus, he accepted—with glee—my offer of a bed for the night. Vernon glanced at me and twisted his lips but didn't protest. We had often put up with law enforcement nonsense and inconvenience.

"Just make sure he stays in the guest room," he whispered to me.

"Are you staying?" I whispered back, crossing my fingers behind me.

He nodded without smiling.

I gave Georgie a toothbrush and soap and pointed him to the room down the hall from mine. It had been renovated along with the rest of the house, and had stood unused for the most of two years. Georgie gazed around the walls and patted the firm mattress. "Better than a hotel! And where's the deputy going to sleep?"

I'd forgotten that Georgie wouldn't know about my relationship with Vernon. I felt a bit embarrassed to actually reveal it to him. He didn't seem old enough—in the head—to know about such things. Surely, I thought, a man with a brain that could figure out bacterial growths in sinkholes and the location of pot fields should be able to comprehend mating humans.

"With me," I said and slipped into the hall, closing the door behind me. I could only imagine the surprise on his face.

A light rain fell, pattering against the oak leaves outside my window. Vernon had shoved a chair under the door knob to my bedroom even though I had turned the lock. "That little turkey is likely to think of something in the middle of the night and burst in here," he said as he pulled me against his swimmer's muscles.

"Vernon?" I stepped back and watched the painful expression on his face. "Forgive me for this morning?"

He grabbed me by the shoulders and squeezed me close. "Damn it, Luanne. I don't like being mad. Can we get past this?"

"I left it miles ago," I said and slipped my arms around his waist.

In spite of the long night and even longer day, my energy soared, and we held each other in bed as two swimmers about to drown in a stormy ocean. Later, as Vernon slept peacefully next to me, I listened carefully for footsteps in the hall. I didn't hear any.

Vernon and I were in the kitchen half an hour before Georgie came down. Most of that time we heard the shower running in the guest bath.

"Either he's super dirty or he's playing with a rubber ducky in there," said Vernon. "If he doesn't turn off that water in ten minutes, I'm knocking on the door."

Twenty minutes later, Georgie came down, his feet clomping hard on the wooden stairs. His hair, still wet, was slicked back against his large head. He had pulled his belt tight, causing the shirt and pants to bulge above and below his waist. He smelled of Chanel.

"Nice bath?" said Vernon.

"Real nice," said Georgie. "You got lots of hot water, and for a swamp house, great water pressure." He sat at the end of the table where I passed him a plate of scrambled eggs and bacon.

"Sleep well?" I asked, and darted a warning glance toward Vernon.

"Like a baby—after I got over thinking about the day, today, I mean." He picked up the bacon, broke it in two pieces and stuffed both inside his mouth. "I've never in my life helped out the police." He grinned and took the fork to his eggs. After two pieces of toast with fig preserves, he stopped to sip coffee. "Where are we going first?"

"The marijuana fields," said Vernon who seemed amazed with this brain kid. He watched every movement of his eating habits.

"Now just be warned," said Georgie, "there might not be any plants growing there. It's just a good place to do it."

"We'll find out," said Vernon. He moved into the living room to call Tony.

"You teach on campus, right?" said Georgie as I poured more coffee. He filled the cup with milk from the carton.

"Linguistics department."

"Yeah, I know the chair of that department."

"How well?" I could see the aging Manny Greenberg with his long hair and bald spot having a conversation with this prodigy of an environmentalist. Manny would be on some save-the-earth tangent; Georgie all the while would think he was asking what would grow where.

"He's part of Green Peace, you know."

"And you?"

"Oh, not me. I just give them scientific data once in a while. Manny sometimes travels with them."

And sometimes smokes with them. He'd had his troubles with "natural" drugs, and these fields of marijuana would be one of the things he'd fight for—not in the open, too easy to lose his position with the university, but secretly he'd support whomever was supplying the stuff.

"You ever see Manny or his friends in the movement smoke weed?"

Georgie didn't hesitate. I might as well have asked if they ever ate candy.

"Sure," he said. "Everybody does it." He looked up quickly. "Not me. I tried it, but it kind of made me sick on my stomach. Besides," he piled preserves on a third piece of toast, "I prefer eating to smoking."

"I'm glad," I said and raised my coffee cup in a private toast to the bags of pot that fell out of his pants pockets.

"Get it together," said Vernon. "Tony's got the warrant. We're off."

Three uniformed deputies accompanied us on the patrol boat to the end of Scrapper Creek then into the woods. One carried a camera. Everyone except Georgie and me carried a gun. I had given him a stick, one of two, I brought along to fend off snakes. Fortunately, he wore rubber galoshes almost all the time. They wouldn't do much for a direct rattlesnake bite, but they'd keep his feet dry. "Wear them around the sites all the time," he had said. "You'd be surprised what I have to step in."

Georgie held his map like Stanley looking for Livingstone and led the way with Tony. Loman and the deputies walked behind them with Vernon and me taking up the rear. Last night's light rain had turned into bright sunshine, threatening to wilt us right down to leaf mold.

"The first clearing is up there," shouted Georgie after we had trudged through heavy brush and pulled off more than one sticky bramble from our pants legs.

"Okay," said Tony, removing the search warrant from his pocket, "wait here." He moved forward, opened the warrant and read it aloud. He then leaned over and propped it against a tree. "We take any samples from the field, we have to note it on the back."

Georgie looked perplexed but asked no questions of this strange requirement of the law.

Trees, at least the tall ones, did not grow in this area. Instead, tall green plants graced the terrain with low scrub in between. All it took for the law men to do was look at the leaves. "Marijuana, all right," said Loman. "Somebody's got some healthy plants here." He broke off a leaf and stuck it in an evidence bag.

"Follow me!" Georgie took off through the head high pot plants and into another growth of trees. After several yards, another cluster of plants. It went on like this until we had located six areas, enough healthy pot patches to furnish someone's wallet for a long time.

"Notify the DEA," said Tony over his cell phone. "But don't call out the copters yet. We've got a search warrant for a barn we need to serve first."

"You'll turn this over to the DEA?" I asked.

"Hell, no!" said Tony. "We handle our own dirt. Just have to notify them."

Georgie grinned. Sweat ran down his face, and he clearly was limping in his uncomfortable boots. But nothing would have turned him away from the adventure of the day. "You want to go to the barn now?"

The walk took us almost all the way back to Scrapper Creek, but turned east just before we saw water. Georgie pushed through the brush, jumped and screamed once when a white oak snake scurried across some leaves, and sounded a "ta-da!" when we reached a clearing clear across the swamp near the road.

"An old barn with some new wood," said Vernon as he pushed against the back door. It gave way. Tony again read the search warrant and placed it in full view atop a sack of hydrilla grass. The inside smelled damp and fecund as though the grass had found a way to grow without water. Something, probably a rat, scurried in the corners and disappeared. The ceiling raised high into the sky, with beams running in rows. In earlier times, tobacco leaves would have hung here to dry and turn brown. Now, their odors lingered and mixed with wetness and the tell-tale spicy pungency.

"Here it is," whispered Georgie. He looked about as though someone would pop up from behind one of the bags. He pointed repeatedly to large garbage bags filled with newly harvested pot, his body bobbing up and down with excitement.

"Okay," said Tony. He made another call, telling the dispatcher to inform the DEA of the barn. "Now let's try and get a warrant for Nettleson's trailer."

"You don't have one already?" I asked.

"Not enough cause. Now that we know about the hydrilla and can connect it with the pot, judge will most likely sign it."

I didn't like this. If Sam Nettleson was involved, he'd surely get wind of the field and barn searches. And, anyone helping him would be long gone, too.

"Who owns this place, by the way?"

"Hanover," said Tony. "He owns lots of river land, including the field of green gold. That doesn't mean he's the one growing this stuff."

"Doesn't mean he's not, either," said Vernon.

Tony turned to Loman. "Anybody located Alice yet?"

Loman collected pot and stuffed it inside more evidence bags. Handing them to a deputy, he checked in with the man heading up the swamp search for Crazy Alice. They had found nothing, and the dogs were only confused with all the water.

"Anybody try the abandoned buildings behind the Ocean Pine? Not the old cabins, but the structures farther back."

Loman stared at Tony with his heavy-lidded eyes. He shrugged and shuffled outside to make another call. The rest of us stood silent, listening to the muffled, one-sided conversation Loman was having with the search team.

"What does Hanover have to say about the search on his land?" I asked.

"What can he say?" Tony said. "The man is in real estate. What happens on his land without his knowledge isn't his fault."

"You think this is without his knowledge?" I waved my hand around the interior of the barn. Its mixture of wet and dry grass with old tobacco roasting odors had begun to settle into a headache. "I need air." The others followed me outside.

"We have to question the man," said Tony as he took a deep inhale of warm, humid air. "Right now he's with his kid, and he's not going anywhere. I got a deputy watching him."

Georgie had begun to wander around the barn. Tony yelled at him. "Hey, kid! Don't touch anything. And try not to walk over any footprints." Georgie stopped in his tracks and turned around military style. With a salute, he came and stood by my side.

"I've been here before," he said. "I found the place, remember?"

"And I am so very grateful," said Tony, attempting sarcasm.

"No, I mean my prints are likely to be in here already."

Tony looked behind him at the imposing structure, its gray boards still rising in honor of the era when tobacco was king. "I'll keep that in mind."

A call came in to Loman's cell phone. "Team found something in one of the buildings. Not in the motel structures, but in an old boat house at the bay." He handed the phone to Tony.

When Tony handed the phone back to Loman, he took a seat on a crate he found outside the barn. The rest of us sat on the grass like Indians waiting for the chief to speak. Tony took a look at Georgie and mentioned a possibility of a sinkhole a few yards away. The man grinned and took off in that direction.

"This is what the team has found. Seems somebody, likely Alice, was living in the boat house. They found it clean and equipped with a cot, some women's dresses and a few other items. And they found an old World War II gun box. No guns inside, but the box is there. Right now, they're going through some papers they found in another box."

"Does the motel own the boat house?" Vernon asked.

"Seems so. The family owns all that land by the bay. Hasn't done much for them lately from the looks of the motel."

"Well," I said, "at least Hanover doesn't own that."

Vernon had tired of Georgie and Tony didn't want him in tow for the next round of investigations. He probably wanted me to take him home, but I shipped him off with a deputy in one of the patrol boats back to the river. The rest of us had to wait for the warrant on Nettleson's trailer. Vernon and I sat on the bank of Scrapper Creek, while Tony and the others dozed in the patrol boat.

"The judge," said the deputy sent to retrieve the warrant, "found the case intriguing. He signed the thing."

At the front of Nettleson's trailer, Tony knocked on the flimsy door. No one answered. We went around back where we were met with the same silence.

"Both doors can be pulled open easily," I said, explaining the locked-up foyer at the back door.

We returned to the front. One deputy stationed himself at the back, gun ready. Tony knocked again. To our surprise, we were met with a muffled female voice that yelled, "Go away!"

Tony yelled back, explaining who he was and that the warrant insisted that she open the door. We waited. After a few minutes, the latch was flipped and the door opened a crack. The first sight was long, straight hair. If I focused on the face, I saw, intermittently, a wide swollen eye staring out at us.

"What do you want?" The voice still sounded muffled even though she spoke through an opening.

"I told you. We have a search warrant for this trailer." Tony held it up alongside his badge ID.

"It's not my place. I'm not supposed to let anyone in while he's—the owner's—not here." She continued to move forward and back from the opening so that glimpses were the only thing we caught of her.

"Doesn't matter, ma'am. Do you want to be arrested for disobeying a court order?" Tony put his hand on the door.

Nothing more was said, but the door came open. The young girl stood back, trying to shadow herself from our view.

"Roxanna!" I gasped at the sight of the battered face. Someone—Nettleson?—had given her a black eye and a split lip. She still wore the halter top and low-cut jeans. "What happened to you?"

The story wasn't pretty, and Roxanna's surly teenage attitude had turned to fear and hurt. She sobbed between words, all the while looking outside to see if Sam was returning.

"He uses us to haul his stuff around," she said and glanced at us sheepishly. "We have this boat, see. It belongs to my cousin. I borrowed it after Tommy smashed up his."

"Did Tommy haul Nettleson's stuff around before he wrecked the boat?" Tony leaned toward her. "And by stuff, do you mean pot?"

The swollen eye attempted to open wide like its mate but it watered instead. She nodded. "He sells it out in the bay."

"And is Patsy helping you?" I asked, remembering the two girls' happy jaunts down the river past my landing.

"Oh, God!" Roxanna put her hand over her mouth, her face showing abject fear.

"What?" said Tony.

"He took her."

"Who took who?"

"Sam," she hiccuped a sob, "he took Patsy away with him. He knocked me around and said to stay here in case somebody tried to rob the place. I couldn't stop him. He's going to hurt her."

Between sobs, she got out the story that Patsy confronted Sam with what she thought had happened—that he had murdered somebody who knew about the marijuana fields. "She doesn't really know who it was, see. She found this old gun. Patsy has brothers who use guns, and she knew the thing had been fired. Sam made a remark that he wouldn't be bothered with that old snoop anymore, and she thought he had killed someone." The reaction to Patsy's accusation was a full beating and threat of torture. "But if he really did kill someone, he might kill her, too."

Roxanna couldn't guess where Sam had taken Patsy. The small girl wouldn't be much of a job for him to handle. Tony and Vernon both believed he took her away to murder her and hide her body. An APB was put out for Nettleson and Patsy.

The search of the trailer turned up small bundles of ready-to-smoke pot, neatly bagged in plastic. Roxanna said it would be placed in a boat and hauled to the bay, and even out to sea in some cases, and sold.

On the way to the hospital, Roxanna sat in the back of a patrol car. She had been read her rights, but she talked a little when asked a question.

"Yeah, we smoked the stuff. Tommy, his step-mom, his dad, Patsy and I. I'm not sure Tommy's dad knew the supplier, but he didn't seem to care. Nor did his step-mom. It was all recreational, they said."

"And do you know where it was grown and harvested?" I asked.

She turned her head to look out the window and nodded, "yeah."

Roxanna's face was patched up in the same hospital where her friend, Tommy, still slept off his drugged stupor. Mr. Hanover paced the waiting room when he wasn't sitting at his bedside. Tony had gone to the room with Loman to warn him of the consequences should he be arrested. The man's only answer was, "Yes, yes. See my attorney."

Vernon and I had left the others to jail Roxanna and stand watch over Hanover. A long day needed the comforts of a good meal at Mama's Table and a cozy night in my swamp house. As usual, the company at the cafe turned out to be about as interesting as the food.

Pasquin, Gavi, and Georgie sat at a table together. There had to be some kind of joking going on, probably at Georgie's expense. We sat at the next table.

"Doesn't that kid have a home to go to?" Vernon whispered to me as we picked up menus.

"I think he's found his calling," I said, and decided on mullet with slaw.

"I think he's found a free ride," added Vernon. "I'll bet Pasquin is paying."

As though he heard us, Pasquin turned to me and said, "You two plan on putting this fellow up again tonight?"

I groaned. Vernon was soon going to find he needed to go home and mow his own lawn or something. I looked at Pasquin and shrugged.

"I thought the deputy was taking you home," I said and looked at Georgie who had begun peeling boiled shrimp, dipping them in sauce and smiling as they went down.

"He got a call to go somewhere. I told him to drop me off at your landing. Mr. Pasquin here was passing in his boat and picked me up."

"It was either that or let him sit on your porch," Pasquin chuckled. He sensed the unease in Vernon. "We had to go back to Portu Landing for some things of Gavi's. That's when we saw him sitting there."

"Dangling his feet in the water," said Gavi. "Like he knew the place."

Resignation set in. If Georgie wanted another night in my guest room, he'd get it, but I vowed the next morning to drive him myself into town and his apartment. The nervousness turned into a sort of homey comfort as we ate the fried seafood and listened to

Pasquin talk about life on the river when he was a kid. He plied us with tales of Cajun parties and how the boys would dance a girl off into the bushes and do his best to take advantage. Her daddy would show up, full of rum, and send the fellow running, bare-assed, into the brush. "Lucky we didn't get snake bit on both cheeks," he said and patted an area near his backside.

"I'll bet you learned a lot about this swamp from having to run from angry papas," I said. "That's how you know where the snake beds are and how not to step on a gator in the dark."

"Yeah," Georgie popped up from his shrimp feast, "just roaming about the territory gets you familiar with all the dangers."

CHAPTER TWENTY

By the time we reached my living room, Georgie had worn just a bit too thin on Vernon. He went silent. I didn't like it, but I also didn't like something that had come out of Georgie's mouth.

"Have a seat at the dining table," I told Georgie. "We need to talk."

Georgie was no fool even though he acted one at times. His grin disappeared and he sat as told. Vernon, sensing something was up, joined us. I placed myself at the corner where I could face Georgie.

"You knew about those marijuana fields before you brought the map out, didn't you?" I waited. He squeezed his lips together and frowned, refusing to say anything.

"You had been all over that area, found the fields, saw Nettleson out there. Like you said, once a person has roamed all over a place, he knows where the dangers are." I leaned into his face. "Not to mention where the goodie bags are." I waited. He continued to frown almost as though he would cry.

"Say something, Georgie. We'll find out sooner or later."

Vernon leaned forward, his face resembling a storm brewing. "You think I need to read you your rights?"

Georgie jumped. "No, no.! It's just that I wasn't sure what to do." He squirmed in his chair. "You're right. I knew the fields were there."

"Tell us about it," Vernon leaned back, his face now in triumphant ease.

Georgie squirmed some more as though he wanted to grind himself into the chair bottom. "That day, when you came looking for information on Nettleson, I remembered him right away. He was a smoker, you know, a joint smoker. Had his sources on the street to buy the stuff. Lots of graduate students got him to buy for them. When he dropped out of the program, there were rumors that he was dealing and making lots of money." He took a deep breath and held on to the arms of the chair. "I was doing the bacteria tests on the project and getting pretty tired of the whole thing. When you came, you got my curiosity up. I went looking for Nettleson. He was easy to find. I watched him come and go to the field and the barn. The hydrilla thing pays him pocket money. He does it for the company that makes the vitamins, and it gives him a sort of cover, I guess. The weed is his own enterprise. I don't know where he sells it or how, but I never saw anyone but him and the two girls out there in those fields."

"And the water tests?"

"Bogus, of course. He's smart and knows how to fool people with that line." He looked sheepishly at me and smiled. "He fooled you, didn't he?"

"Why didn't you tell the sheriff about the fields?" Vernon leaned toward him again.

"Well, I did, sort of. I told you about the barn and I pointed out the possible areas on the map."

"You invented your own scenario," I said. "You knew about Nettleson's trailer and what he kept inside it, didn't you?"

He didn't answer.

"I mean just what if you went inside it once while he wasn't there and stuffed all those military pockets full of little plastic bags of weed? You'd make a nice little sum on campus, wouldn't you?"

Georgie pulled off his glasses and squinted at me. He started to say something and stopped.

"What this means, Georgie, if you are now really telling the whole truth, is that we can't trust you anymore. You've deceived us for what— adventure? Whatever it was, you've placed yourself in about the same situation as a suspect." Vernon lay his sheriff's badge on the table between them.

"Oh, please," Georgie begged. "I'll make up for it. I got lots of knowledge about these swamps. Let me help, please."

"Talk," said Vernon and folded his arms atop the table.

Georgie replaced his glasses and looked at me for help. I nodded to indicate he should open up or else.

"I followed Nettleson, first because I saw him in the pot fields. But then I watched him take those two girls there one day. He was mad at them for something. Kept telling them they'd have to do the work their friend did before he killed himself in his boat. I figured he was talking about Tommy Hanover." Georgie looked at me again and asked for a glass of water.

"Not yet," said Vernon. "You followed Nettleson and the girls?"

He nodded. "To the fields. He made them harvest the stuff. You could tell they weren't used to that kind of work and the weather was hot. They complained a lot. He slapped the tall one. She cried, and he just slapped her again and told her to work on a certain spot. He grabbed the small one and dragged her off to the next field. It was easy, you see, to skirt into the woods and follow them from a distance. She tried to argue with him, even screamed some nasty words, but he socked her, too, and she started to work. And you know what he did? He sat down and smoked a joint!"

The room became quiet. "So, Georgie," said Vernon, "you are quite the voyeur. What exactly did you plan to do with this knowledge?"

"Nothing, really. I know it was round about, but I did let the law know about the pot."

"Were you, by chance, planning to contact Nettleson with your knowledge of his exploits? Maybe ask for a little bit of the pot money to keep quiet?"

Georgie gasped and slid his chair back a few inches. "Never! Don't accuse me of that."

Vernon smiled. The Cheshire Cat would have been proud. "You're going back to your apartment right now," he said. "I'll drive you. And tomorrow morning, you're going to relate in detail all about your tailing and spying to Detective Amado. Is that clear?"

There was no quarrel. Georgie stood up and headed for the front door. I smiled and pulled Vernon aside. "You might want to get a search warrant for his room." I said. A look passed between us. He sensed I was telling him more but he shouldn't ask.

Vernon couldn't return for the night. He had called Tony with the news about Georgie's added information, and Tony wanted him at the hospital. Roxanna had opened her mouth wide while she lay on that bed.

"We're looking for Nettleson big time now," said Vernon as he drank coffee. He had stopped by my place at five in the morning on his way home and to bed. Stubble grew on his tanned jaws, and his usual bright eyes were dotted with red streaks. "Tony's got a search team in the swamp."

"And the search team for Alice?" I handed him toast.

"Tony thinks she could be dead. From what Roxanna told us, Nettleson is capable."

"Tell me," I said and poured orange juice.

Vernon took a deep breath. It didn't do much to overcome his fatigue and I could feel his age catching up with his strength. It made me feel overwhelmingly sad for a moment.

"The three of them—two girls and the Hanover kid—had all

too willingly been coaxed into helping Nettleson with his project.
They saw money, yes, but it was more the adventure and dealing
with weed, having it to pass around among their rich friends. Tommy
had a boat, something Nettleson needed to get his sales on the
seas." Vernon stopped and sipped his coffee. "You got a wet cloth?"

He rubbed his face with a kitchen towel soaked in cold water.
"Roxanna said he had tried to connect with some fishermen in his
early tries. One old guy took him out a few times and watched him
sell to some boaters he met out there. The old man got wind of the
money he could make and threatened to go to the law if Nettleson
didn't cut him in. That's when Sam took action."

"Otis Reynolds?"

"Yeah. He went to pick up the goods from Nettleson at the end
of Scrapper Creek. While he was off the boat, Nettleson did something to the engine. Otis comes back and can't start the thing. He
goes into the bilge, and Nettleson shoots him from above."

"Right in the top of the head."

"And with a stolen gun, evidently. That's another thing Roxanna
said. He'd found a gun in a crazy old lady's place and took it. Bragged
that nobody would ever be able to trace it." He stopped to eat some
bacon and drink the juice. "Knocked a hole in Otis' boat and let it
sink along with the body."

"Why didn't Nettleson buy himself a boat?"

"Too risky, I guess. He'd need a license. When he found the
Hanover kid and his two girls, he figured he'd got himself a slave
force. That's what the girls became."

"Were the girls used in other ways?"

Vernon nodded. "Roxanna said it was all fun at first. Orgies for
the four of them. But Nettleson got brutal after awhile, even more
so after the Hanover accident. Both girls wanted out, but Sam threatened them. At least that's what she's saying."

"And where is Patsy?"

"With Nettleson, or dead. That stupid Georgie doesn't know how lucky he is. If Nettleson had caught him snooping around, he would have blown a hole in his skull, too."

"Then Jacob and Barley Ben…"

Vernon nodded. "The two of them must have stumbled across the fields or the barn. Nettleson wouldn't have let either go free. But, Roxanna doesn't know anything about them. Guess Nettleson hadn't gotten around to bragging about them yet." He chuckled a little, too weary to laugh out loud. "We're getting the search warrant on Georgie's place. You think he got some of the pot and planned to sell it, don't you?"

"You could sleep here, you know," I said, ignoring the question, and stroked Vernon's bald head.

"I need to see about my mail and stuff. You better get into town and buy yourself a new cell phone." He wiped his mouth, pulled me close, then rose slowly and headed out of my corner of the swamp.

I lay down on the sofa. The air conditioning hum from the heat pump came on frequently, lulling me into a sleep that lasted until someone knocked on the door at nine.

"Harry?" I dreaded dealing with this broken man, and immediately felt a pang of guilt.

"I just dropped by to tell you the latest." He grinned and looked confident for the first time in months.

"Couldn't you have phoned? It's a long way out here."

His smile faded. "It's good news. I thought you might like to share it."

"Harry, look, you're making things pretty awkward for me."

He stood there, a hang dog look of confusion on his face.

"Okay," I said. "Come in and tell me the news, but you've got to give me some space."

"It's Vernon, isn't it?" He sat on the sofa. "He's making waves."

"Harry, he has a right to make waves. We're an item, a pretty big item. You, well, you just tend to demand too much. And it's obvious I can't help you. I don't know why you keep running to me with this diving phobia."

"I guess I won't be from now on," he said. "That's what I wanted to tell you about. I'm in therapy. A group thing with other divers. I never knew there was such a thing until the guy who runs the hyperbaric chamber told me about it. The doctor holds it right there in the hospital. Chalker is in the group. You know, the guy Hanover hired. He had a heart attack in the water and vows never to swim again."

"That's wonderful, Harry. You'll stick with it, right?"

"Yeah, of course." He sat back and stared at me, a sadness reflecting in his eyes. "No chance you'd like to celebrate with dinner?"

"No chance." I stared back.

He sighed. "Well, just one other thing. Chalker talked a lot about his rescue in the first session. He was kind of vague about some old woman pulling him on shore. Said she had long gray hair. I figured he was either hallucinating or it was Crazy Alice."

"Crazy Alice?" I stopped to think about the time element. Could Nettleson have murdered Alice after that incident? Perhaps, but maybe not. She was cagey, like Georgie, and maybe had dodged his bullets.

Harry stood. He made a gesture toward me as though he wanted to hug me. I stood apart and refused to give him the opportunity. At the door, he turned to me.

"I'll get it back, Luanne. Diving is something I don't want to lose. I will get it back."

Harry drove away in his battered VW. If he ever dove again, someone else would have to be his buddy. I stood on the porch long after his car disappeared from sight. The sounds of the forest sang around me and for a moment I let my mind go numb. I finally moved back into the living room, into the civilized air condition and the comfort of my cocoon.

From the front porch came the sound of a screen slamming and a dog barking.

"Plato!" I said as I let him into the living room. He wagged his tail and rolled over for a belly scratch. "How did you get back here?"

"Came with me," said Pasquin who climbed the front steps. "Took Gavi back to Portu Landing. Guess the old swamp dog had had enough of the other side of town. Hopped on the boat with me."

"Gavi isn't staying with you any longer?"

"No, that old man ain't happy in a real house. He's used to his trailer and the outdoors. He's about like this old dog, got to keep sniffing in the woods." Pasquin leaned over to scratch Plato's ears.

We sat in the cool of the living room. Pasquin sipped some tea and propped his feet on an ottoman.

"You ever wonder about this old dog?"

"You or the one on the floor?"

Pasquin glared at me, but the twinkle in one eye let me know I hadn't insulted my elder too much. "Why, the one with all the fur, ma'am."

"I wonder about him all the time. He survives out here in spite of gators and crazies running around with guns, not to mention black bears and rattlesnakes."

"More than that. He never gets fleas." Pasquin leaned over with two hands and began parting the short fur. Plato turned his head and panted, loving the grooming that all animals seemed to relish.

"I've never found a single one on him."

I moved closer and focussed on the dog's bare skin under the fur. "You're joking old man. He gets both fleas and ticks." I brushed Plato's fur with one hand.

"Ever see one? I haven't and I spent some time at that camp looking."

"Well, if you're right, it's good. I won't get any eggs in the rugs."

We relaxed and let Plato fall asleep at Pasquin's feet. He knew us, knew Gavi and Vernon, and Pasquin's strange friend, Edwin. His trust was complete, as though he could tell us he may be off for a while, but he'd be back.

"Never saw a domestic animal learn the woods so good," said Pasquin. "You planning on giving me something better than this?" He held his tea in the air.

"I don't have any Cajun brew. You want lemonade?"

He nodded and passed me the glass.

When Pasquin had a cold glass in one hand, and a wedge of pound cake in the other, he leaned back in his chair. "Some people are like this old dog." He glanced at me and grinned. "The one on the floor."

"You mean they know how to survive the swamp? In that case, I'd say you and he are pretty near brothers."

"Yep, could be." He took a bite of the cake and rested the remaining piece on a napkin in his lap. "I'm referring, however, to Miss Alice Calder."

"If she really has survived. She may be dead."

"Yeah, just like Jacob and old Barley Ben. But if she ain't, she's a human sister to this beast." He nudged Plato who wagged a tail but didn't open his eyes. "And she's pulpy in the head, to boot."

"She ran away from her fellow humans," I said, "but made peace with the swamp. Strange. Rejection must have played a role in her life. That father of hers. She thought he needed a son-in-law, which she couldn't produce."

"Been trying ever since, before and after the old man shot a hole in his head." Pasquin finished off the cake and sipped loudly on the lemonade.

"That's what happened to Tommy, I'll bet," I said. "She must have been around that night when the teenagers were racing the boat in a big circle, high on Nettleson's pot. When the manatee interfered and they went flying, it was Alice who pulled Tommy from the water. Just like she pulled Hanover's diver out later. She somehow got Tommy back to that old trailer and kept him there. All that talk about 'I got me a man' was for real. She really had got her a man in the form of Tommy Hanover. And with sleeping pills she wasn't about to let him get away."

"You sound about as crazy as she is," said Pasquin. "Only thing is, you could be right."

"I'll bet on it." I ate a piece of the pound cake and poured myself a lemonade. We sat in silence. This was our habit, inherited from a long line of Southerners who sat on porches and rocked long after dark, saying nothing for an eternity, then bringing up some subject that would end quickly. We were like planets who passed each other in orbit, comfortable with the universe.

"I've got to go into town and buy a cell phone replacement. Mine is floating in a sinkhole."

"Come on with me to Mama's Table for lunch. You can find a phone in Fogarty Spring."

"Not the one I want, but maybe I'll see what the store can do." Mama's Table appealed to me more than getting into the car and driving, in nearly hundred degree heat, to a big electronics store. "Maybe they'll deliver it."

The miracle of modern economy made it true. The clerk offered to replace the phone I lost, with the same number, and deliver it to me at Mama's Table. "We've heard a lot about you, Miz Fogarty," she drawled on the phone. "I'm sure you need a phone in the line of work you do." She knew about the adjunct diving; I doubt she knew about the linguistics teaching that really paid the bills.

"Life cooperates sometimes," I said and piled into Pasquin's motor boat. We took umbrellas and had to open them up not long after pushing off the landing. A light rain came down, making tattoo marks on the clear river water. Plato had refused to come with us, moving instead to the front porch and flopping into a rocking chair.

Mama's Table had its supply of locals and fishermen for lunch. The odors of fried fish and hush puppies filled the air. But the heat told us to order the seafood salad and drink iced tea that condensed on the glasses and made rings on the plastic table tops. Pasquin dumped tobasco onto his greens.

As the human traffic faded away, we sat and chatted with Mama. Calvin cleaned tables until Mama told him to sit down and rest a spell. He began to tell us about the search of his parents' property.

"They showed up with a search warrant, but Daddy said they didn't need it, to go ahead and look at anything back there. The only place they found anything was in that boat house. My grandfather rented canoes and stuff there once. The boat slip is still there and most likely could still be used. It was the room over the top that Alice used for her living quarters. Didn't have much, it seemed. But she had a cot. Nobody knew she was there, or cared, until now." He sipped on a glass of tea Mama had poured for him.

"Did you ever track down the guests and ask if they were missing their sleeping pills?"

"The sheriff did, and you know what, they all were missing them but didn't associate our motel with the loss. They figured they just misplaced them or left them behind somewhere. Guess old Alice had herself a little box of drugs. Her own stash, you might say."

"Any idea where Alice is now?"

"None," he said. "She disappeared and doesn't come back to the boat house. They've got her place surveilled." He leaned over and whispered this to me.

"I figured they would," I whispered back.

Mama stood to wait on a new customer who had come in. "If you ask me, that old woman is floatin' in a spring cave about now."

CHAPTER TWENTY-ONE

The phone took its time in arriving. We had sat inside the cafe and had some custard pie until we could stand the hard booth no longer. We moved to the landing just outside the cafe, but that got just as hard. Finally, we moved to the cushions of Pasquin's boat and dozed as it gently rocked in the water.

Thunder rumbled just as the truck pulled up and a red-haired pubescent male tumbled out of the cab. He had a box under his arm as he darted toward the cafe entrance.

"Is that my phone?" I yelled over the rumble.

The kid looked confused, but finally turned and dashed toward me. "I got deliveries all over this county from the store. You want to sign right here?" He pulled out a crumpled print-out and handed me a ball point pen.

I waved the box in the air as Pasquin rose from his reclining position in the boat. In a sudden gust of wind, his straw hat tumbled off his head and onto the landing.

"We got to run!" He stood up, leaped onto the landing with the agility of a man half his age and retrieved his hat. I followed him up the stairs and into the cafe just as the heavens opened up. It could have been a giant fire hose from the sky. For half an hour, we couldn't see the bottom of the stairs, much less Pasquin's boat.

"Got the place all to yourselves," said Mama. "Coffee or tea?"

We sipped tea until we could float. Calvin sprayed and cleaned the tables and chairs and pushed a broom across the floor. He kept checking his watch.

"Can't go nowhere in this downpour," said Mama. "Your parents will understand."

"Might not even be raining down on the bay," he said.

"That's true," Mama turned her hips in the chair, making a squeaking sound with the skin on the backs of her legs against the plastic.

"You know anything about Alice Calder's family?" I asked. "I know we've brought her up before, but I just wondered if there were ever any rumors."

"Rumors all over the swamp, honey," said Mama. "Gossip gets started around here and grows like toadstools after a rain."

"Tell me some."

She chuckled. "Now not one story can be proved. The best one is that the old Alice has turned into a swamp witch, somebody who can turn a man into a frog that no princess' kiss will ever reconvert." She poured more tea and made a comment about having to use the bathroom all night long. "Some people thought she might cure skin diseases with herbs and things. The old lady took to collecting various grasses and roots and passing them off as cures. Gave one old geezer who had rheumatism the worst case of poison oak you ever saw on an old man's skin. Nearly killed him."

Pasquin laughed. "I knew that old thief. Deserved what he got. Even tried to sue her but the judge told him he ought to be committed for using the stuff. Now I do know what she tried to do to Edwin one time. Think she wanted to make him her 'man' and he wasn't having any of it. She didn't like the snakes and said if she ever came to live there, he'd have to get rid of them. Said it wasn't natural to hold a live snake in a cage. Makes them all mad and evil like. Bite you for sure that way." He stopped to gulp down half a glass of tea and laugh at his story. "About two years ago, she goes by his place late at night and cuts open every one of his cages. Snakes crawled all over the swamp that night, dancing for joy at being freed." He held out the glass for a refill. "That's when she decided he wasn't going to be her man after all. He didn't get mad, or run after her. He sat down and cried. Like a baby, he opened up them tear ducts and just howled." Pasquin let out a laugh and Mama joined him.

"She don't seem to care how old these men are, does she?" said Mama. "Young man like Edwin could be her son."

"Cry baby," said Pasquin.

"And then there's the time she embarrassed the tourists," said Mama. "Seems they had rented canoes, about four of them. Each member of the family had his own. They went rowing off down the river, hoping to see an alligator on the banks or a manatee swimming beside them. Instead, they went into that cul-de-sac in the river bend, the one where the oak nearly stretches across to the other side. Water is real clear just beyond that tree. Old Alice uses it to bathe in. Jerks off every stitch of clothes—and she doesn't wear much under those dresses—and romps around in the water. Her long gray hair floats around behind her. Bet she looks like the mermaid's grandma!" Mama tilted her head back and laughed. "I think I'll join her when I get her age. Why not, these old hips could shake up a few tourists." She headed off for the bathroom.

"The tree that covers the river?" I turned to Pasquin. "That's way up the river. Kind of in a grove of nice trees."

Pasquin nodded. "Government property. Too pretty to let somebody build a house on it."

"If she bathes there, Pasquin…" I looked at him.

"You want to take a ride up that way, don't you?"

He waited his turn for the bath room then motioned for me to follow him out the door. "You always got a job for this old man."

We traveled up the river, leaving the little town of Fogarty Spring behind and headed toward the state park where glass bottom boats took northerners on a tour of the deepest fresh water spring caves in the world.

The houses on shore began to give way to lush trees that had stood and flourished for hundreds of years. Their limbs draped across the pristine water, some so low that their leaves bounced on the surface when the breezes blew. Their roots were back on shore and clung firmly to the spot where some Indian had long ago stumbled across an acorn.

"Tree is right here," Pasquin said and slowed the engine. He guided the boat around the limbs and came to a halt in deep water that seemed engulfed between competing giant oaks. A small patch of shore line led to a clearing on a small hill.

"I'll have to swim to get to shore," I said.

"You planning on being long up there?" Pasquin moved as close as he could to the bank.

"No, and I'll be wet. Hope I don't meet anyone." I pulled off my shoes and watch. "You hold onto the phone."

"How come you ain't got on your swimming suit?"

"Never thought I'd be diving today," I said. Normally, I'd wear a suit under my clothes. This time, I threw my legs over the side and hit the cold water fully dressed. The effect was an immediate feeling of being pulled down. I got over it and swam to shore.

"I'll be back shortly," I said, not really knowing if this was true. Alice Calder could be far back into the woods, or nowhere around here, but if there were signs, I'd like to find them.

The walk would have been a nature lover's dream. A sandy path led between pines and oaks straight to a tiny cabin. In another time, one might have mistaken it for an outhouse. It was nestled among three pines so that a little yard of needles circled the structure. I did the proper thing and knocked on the door but no one answered. There were no windows, but I was betting anyone could have seen through a couple of gaps in the wall boards. I moved to one side and stepped onto something hard. Brushing back the needles, I saw the rocks piled in a little nest. I shoved the stones aside and loosened the dirt. The skeleton of a squirrel lay in the shallow hole, the remnants of a wild flower under its chin. Walking around the cabin, I found the same formation at each corner. I didn't look for more bones, but some poor animal must have been honored at each site.

There was no back door. I took a deep breath and pushed on the front. It moved inward; something fell to the floor. I bent over to pick up piece of red cloth that someone had placed in the door, probably to signal that an intruder had been here. Passing inside, I had to let my eyes adjust to the darkness. The interior cleanliness surprised me. There was no dust. An old army cot sat folded against the wall, its sheets folded neatly on a shelf above it. A wooden box that from the outside looked like a toy storage box held folded underclothes and two muu-muu style dresses. A board lay over the box, covering half the top and holding mirrors, brushes, and jars of creams. Some bricks lay piled next to the door. Instead of candles, there were four flashlights standing on end. "Wise," I thought. "No chance of burning the place down." There were no signs of food or ways of making it, nor of a portable bathroom. "She eats some-where else and most likely uses the forest for a toilet." Above me, the roof looked solid. It was covered in tin on the outside and probably made a hell of a noise when it rained, but let no water inside.

The silence of the place seemed profound. The woman would sleep well here, safe in her tight little cabin. Suddenly, the quiet was interrupted by a familiar bark. A brown muzzle stuck through the half open door.

"Plato? How in the world did you get here?"

The dog wagged his tail and dropped at my feet until I rubbed his tummy. Then he found a corner and plopped down as though he had been living here always.

"You little scoundrel," I said. "You know Alice, don't you?"

He wagged his tail and panted. If only dogs could talk.

I tried to replace the red cloth. It wouldn't work, I was sure. If Alice had been clever enough to use it in the first place, she would have known which way she put it in the door. I roamed a while but could find no other paths in or out of the forest. Plato followed me, often looking up as if to ask what I was doing.

At the shore, I figured Plato would have to abandon us again. Pasquin couldn't bring the boat close to the edge here. But the dog didn't run. He jumped into the water with me and swam right to the boat. I shoved him over the side where he took a seat next to Pasquin.

"You found something," he said and patted the dog's head.

"Alice must use a boat to get here," I said as I crawled into the boat. "Unless there is some other wild woman living in the swamp, this is her place."

"Wild women all over the area," said Pasquin. "None so wild as to live with the forest haints, but wild just the same." He nodded in my direction.

"Feral woman, now that's a new species," I said and punched the numbers to inform Tony of the little cabin. Some spot inside me hated doing that, because it would mean the destruction of a nest that Alice had built for herself. A place where she had said little rituals over the graves of dead animals. It seemed she built those rock formations wherever she found something dead, one at her old homestead and where Jacob's body was discovered.

Before we reached my landing, the cell phone rang again. It was

Tony.

"You need to come into town, Luanne. We're talking to Georgie."

"You found marijuana in his room," I said as I entered the sheriff's department conference room. "How about that." I smiled to myself as I sat at the square table.

"He wants to talk and maybe cut a deal. Says he's got some real gritty stuff to tell." Vernon moved to a chair beside me. "I figured he'd talk more if you were here, or at least he'd be more likely to tell the truth."

"And his lawyer?"

"Court appointed. They don't pay much on those graduate student grants."

Tony entered the room. He glanced my way but said nothing. Georgie followed with a young man who had to be a month out of law school. Loman stood in the corner as there wasn't another chair.

After the preliminaries with the recorder, Georgie went through the same story he had told us about the barn and the fields. Only this time, he added some details.

"Like I said, it was easy to watch from the woods. Nettleson wasn't too smart. He didn't think anyone could see what he was doing. I hid in the scrub and watched him and the girls gather the weed and shove it into thirty gallon bags. Most of the time he'd make one girl stay in one patch and drag the other off to another one. That's where he'd—you know—have them. Right there on the ground in the weed patch. He liked to slap them around a little first. Make them submissive. They'd give in and he'd have sex with them. Right after, they had to get up and start harvesting. That's when he'd smoke one himself. Don't know why they put up with it. I mean why didn't the other girl run away?"

I leaned forward, feeling the blood rise to my neck. "Why didn't you do something, Georgie? Why didn't you come to the girls' rescue? Or did you get your jollies, too, watching a little porno reality in the field?"

He turned to his lawyer whose face went pale and began to sweat. "We have an agreement here," he said. "My client talks only on terms of leniency."

I leaned back. My tendency was to accuse him of jacking off in the swamp, of getting pleasure from the whole sadistic scene. Tony's tight jaw and glare told me to keep quiet.

"And you took some marijuana packets from Nettleson's trailer to sell?" asked Vernon.

Georgie gulped and looked at the attorney who nodded.

"Yeah, I did." He jerked off his glasses and squinted in the bright room. "I never did anything like that before, but I knew what some of the students were paying for the stuff. I never really sold it, though. Never got up the nerve to offer it to anyone."

We left the odd little Georgie Porgie, weeping through his squinty eyes, not only because he was being held but because he had likely ruined his scientific career. I figured he'd survive. With his genius, some firm would hire him without even looking at his one venture into selling dope and spying on people doing nasty things.

Vernon and Tony had to see Tommy Hanover at the hospital. I decided to tag along. When Tony breathed in heavily in anticipation of protesting, I reminded him of who found the kid. He stormed out the door; Vernon and I followed.

"I'll sit in the back," I said and climbed into Tony's car. Vernon moved into the front. Before we pulled out, Loman joined me in the back seat.

Tommy Hanover lay on the hospital bed, his eyes staring into ours as though he hadn't the slightest idea anyone was really there. His lawyer and his father's lawyer stood behind Mr. Hanover. All three stared at us, but it was clear they knew we were there.

"He remembers nothing," said Mr. Hanover. He had on a dark suit with a tie today.

"And you, sir," said Tony, "what do you remember?"

He whipped his head around to his lawyer. The seasoned man, at least sixty, stepped closer to the bed. "My client will not be interviewed in the presence of his son. The boy is sick enough as is."

"Let's head to a waiting room then," said Tony. "And only your lawyer. Tommy's can stay here in case he decides to jog his memory." Tony's sarcasm shot through the room. We followed him outside where he asked a uniform deputy to clear the waiting room.

Once the nurse found a place for the one family sitting in the waiting room, we all filed in, the uniform keeping watch at the door.

"This is an interview, sir," said Tony. "You haven't been read your rights—not yet."

The lawyer nodded and took a seat next to his client. The two men sat stiffly, their suits matching.

"We've found things on your land, mainly marijuana groves, Mr. Hanover. What is your comment on that?"

The man cleared his throat but the lawyer put out a hand and spoke for him. "Mr. Hanover owns lots of land in this county and the next two. It's open land, much of it without fences. If someone wanders on it and commits a crime, he cannot be held responsible. In fact, if you held anyone responsible in that regard, you'd have most of the county in jail."

"His son was aiding and abetting in the sale of pot, sir." Tony's olive skin reddened.

"You don't know that for a fact. You have only the word of one teenage girl. You'll have to find proof. And," he moved to the edge of his chair, "even if you can find proof, it in no way condemns my client. What his son has done—and his son has turned eighteen—is not his responsibility."

The interview ended in frustration for everyone. Mr. Hanover was obstinate. No confession would come out of his mouth.

"It's Nettleson we really want," said Tony as we stood on the hospital steps. "Hanover would be a good catch, but Nettleson is the prize."

CHAPTER TWENTY-TWO

I drove the distance to my house alone. The road seemed dark and lonely, and I knew that out there somewhere, Sam Nettleson had Patsy. Maybe he had dug a hole and buried her by now or more likely dumped her body into a remote spring. Did he put Alice in one, too? I couldn't shake the feeling that maybe Alice had outfoxed him. She could still be running about the forest, barefoot and loose haired and free.

I called Pasquin as soon as I arrived at home. "Let's just ride up and down the river lanes. Maybe we'll see or hear something about Alice." He agreed.

"Tired of sitting in this cold air conditioning anyway," he said. Within the hour, he picked me up at my landing. Plato sat in the boat with him.

"Old dog was sleeping on my landing. I invited him along."

"I doubt you could have made him stay behind if he wanted to come," I said and scratched Plato's ears. "Let's ride the other way, toward the little cabin we found before."

Plato sat on the back seat on his haunches, his nose constantly sniffing the air. If other people's dogs liked to sniff out the car window, mine sniffed river air. Could he smell a gator three feet below us or a deer on shore? I watched his scruffy brown ears blow in the breezes kicked up by the movement of the boat. He squinted his eyes from time to time, but mostly they were wide open.

About halfway to the old cabin, we passed one of the many old landings on the river. Three boats were tied up there. Plato began to bark in their direction.

"Let's pull up beside them," I said.

Pasquin guided the boat slowly past each one. They seemed harmless motor boats, probably belonging to fishermen who camped back in the woods. But, Plato barked again, this time standing on the seat and staring a bit downstream. Another motor boat was tied to an old post that stuck out of the shallow water. I motioned Pasquin in that direction.

As soon as we pulled beside it, Plato hopped across and planted himself on a cushion that rested behind the one seat. The boat wasn't new.

"Now just what makes him so at home in this tub?" asked Pasquin.

I grabbed the side of the boat and pulled us closer. Next to Plato's pillow was a pile of rolled up plastic bags. I touched the end of one and let it unroll. Out dropped a flowered muu-muu and a bag of hard candy. I pulled up another bag; a woman's underpants fell out along with packages of beef jerky. Leaning over, I saw the now familiar specimen box jammed against one side. It felt heavy and when I opened it, I found pebbles inside, hundreds of them.

"Little memorial rocks in one of Nettleson's boxes," I said. "This is Alice's boat, Pasquin. She's around somewhere. Plato is familiar with it because he has been on rides in it, just like he has been in her cabin." I skirted the shore with my eyes.

"She ain't necessarily around, Luanne. Nettleson could have stolen it after he did away with her." Pasquin's eyes darted the shores, too, perhaps remembering what Sam had done to other old river men. "Let the sheriff know about this. They got search parties."

When we arrived at Pasquin's landing, it was almost twilight.

"You want to come in for a bite of Cajun shrimp? I cooked up some last night. Too many for this old man to eat up."

I followed him inside his hot house. He switched on the window air-conditioning and a faint cool draft forced itself into the rooms. Pasquin pulled out a pan and dumped the cooked shrimp into it. I could smell the hot sauce as he pushed them around in the hot pan. After portioning them onto two plates, he put on the coffee pot to make his strong brew.

"How can you sleep nights after drinking this stuff?" I filled my coffee with milk.

"Never have trouble sleeping unless there's too much noise."

"Your air conditioner isn't exactly a soft murmur." I had to get a glass of water to wash down the spicy shrimp.

"I turn that thing off. Can't sleep with a draft over me, and I need to hear the swamp sounds." He pointed to a window. "Got good screens."

"Humidity doesn't get to you?" I remembered my own house before I had it wired for central air. Breezes out of the hot swamp were rare and I'd wake up sweating down my back where it made contact with the bedding. There was never a question of covers. I never cooled off the entire night, and to make things worse, there was at least one mosquito per hour that buzzed my head.

"Comforts me," he said and pushed hot shrimp into his mouth.

By the time we finished, and I insisted on helping him clean up, it was dark.

"I'll walk home," I said. "Just lend me a flashlight."

"You sure?"

"I've done it before plenty of times. And if anyone is going to shoot at me again, they could do it just as easily while I sat in a boat. You've done enough work for one day, old man. Turn off your air-conditioner and get some sleep."

"Ha! This old Cajun will stay up with the hootie owls."

I grabbed the flashlight and headed for the path through the swamp that would take me to my front door. I had traveled this way for years. The moon was out and the skies had cleared. I'd need the light mostly for the path itself.

I had gone nearly three fourths the distance and had just turned on the light, when I heard footsteps coming rapidly behind me. Twisting sharply, I ducked behind a tree and hoped I wouldn't step on a rattler out looking for his mousie dinner.

"Luanne!" Pasquin's familiar voice whispered through the trees. "You there?"

"What's wrong? You nearly scared me to death." I stepped in front of a panting old man who had come out without his straw hat.

"There's a ruckus going on out back of the tool shed."

I turned toward his house again and headed back. Pasquin followed, his steps as silent as any primitive Indian stalking a nighttime enemy. As the trees cleared and the moonlight took over, I clicked off the flashlight. We stopped dead and listened. Suddenly, odd forms rushed from around the side of the tool shed and dashed inside. We heard a plastic trash can fall, taking with it some tools. Someone cried out as though in sharp pain. Then another voice took over.

"Hush, hush." The voice, a feminine one began to sing. "Mary knows what to do, Mary knows what to do." Over and over again, the song came out like a lullaby. It wasn't loud, but in the silence of the swamp, the sound carried.

"That's Alice!" I whispered. "It's the same thing she sang when we found Jacob." I moved toward the shed and was about to turn on the light when running steps came out of the swamp from a different direction.

"Back here," said Pasquin and pulled me to the house side of the shed. "Somebody's coming."

A flashlight shined through the trees, bobbing along with the running steps. In a flash of a second, a man burst from the trees and stood at the entrance to the shed. From our position, we could see his profile. He shined his light inside and focused on the huddled figure of Alice Calder. Her hair had fallen around her like a protective spider web. She squatted, her loose dress hiked over knees and the ragged sandals balancing her plump figure. A lump of groaning material lay at her side. She stroked the hair.

"Don't you worry, Mary knows what to do. Mary does the right thing." She had begun to sing again. Her eyes wide and unblinking stared into the light coming from the man's hand.

"Just bring her out of there, you old bitch. I've got a gun." The man moved the flashlight slightly to pull a pistol from his belt.

"Nettleson!" I whispered to Pasquin. He had silently put his fingers around the handle of a hoe left at the side of his shed.

Nettleson looked up as though he had heard something, but turned back to the women in the barn. "Just bring her out and nobody will get hurt."

"You already hurt her!" Alice's voice screamed into the calm of the night. "You can't have her." She leaned over to the girl and patted her head.

Nettleson moved his light to the girl's face. Patsy sat up now, her body a bruised, torn and bloody mess. She began to rock like an autistic child.

"She's hurt!" Alice spat this out like venom. She stood and shaded her eyes.

"It's a gun, old woman, see!" Nettleson shined the light directly on the pistol.

"That's mine!" She moved forward, one hand still shading her eyes, the other folded behind her. "My daddy gave it to me. You stole it!"

"Yeah," Nettleson laughed, "you creepy cow. I stole it. Right out of that boat house you called a home."

"What did you say?"

"I said I stole it, creepy cow." Nettleson was yelling now. He had moved the gun to his side.

"You don't call me a cow!" Alice pulled her hand from behind her and raised it, using the free hand to balance the pistol she aimed at Nettleson.

He must have seen it, in the second it took to blast away his vision forever. Alice's pistol fired once, shocking the forest into flight, and throwing Nettleson backward with a hole in his head.

Pasquin and I froze. We watched as Alice stared at the light on the ground and the body that was now a shadow in the moonlight. She held her gun down by her side and walked toward Nettleson. Picking up the pistol he had dropped, she walked back inside the shed and placed them in front of her. "My pistols. My daddy gave them to me. You had no right to take them." She let them sit and turned her attention back to Patsy who had tried to crawl away when the shot went off. "They are mine, you know."

I handed the cell phone to Pasquin and motioned for him to call the sheriff. I moved toward the shed. In a voice as calm as I could muster, I said, "Alice, you have your man now."

She didn't jump or grab the guns. She looked up at me and smiled. "I do, don't I?"

"You do. Would you like to come inside where you can rest and make some tea?"

She looked at her hands and felt her hair. "I seem a mess. Maybe I'd better clean up first."

"Yes, come and use the bathroom. You want to look your best."

Alice stood up. She took her long hair in both hands and held it away from her face. "Could you braid it for me."

"I'd be happy to." She walked with me inside Pasquin's house.

We sat in Tony's office, surrounded by clutter piled on chairs. A deputy took the seat behind the desk and opened his notebook. "We have to work in here," he said. "They're using all the conference rooms right now." It was time to give a statement.

Pasquin saw me coming with Alice in tow and pointed to the phone. I motioned for him to leave the house. He stayed with Patsy and Nettleson. I took Alice inside where she sat in a chair, sighing as though she hadn't felt so comfortable in years. I went to her back and began braiding the strands of gray hair, pulling out brambles and leaves as I worked. She hummed a lot, even closed her eyes. I took my time with the braids. When I heard the boat sirens on the river, I tried talking to her to keep her relaxed. It didn't seem necessary. She must not have heard the sirens at all.

The rest of my statement consisted of paramedics taking Alice away. She didn't mind that, either. Two men escorting her to a nice white boat. She slung her braids about as she walked away with them.

Nettleson was beyond help. Alice had a second chance to avenge someone calling her a cow, and she didn't miss this time. Patsy, beaten and in shock, took a police boat ride to the hospital. She'd later tell how Nettleson had brutalized her and left her to retrieve his pistol. She was sure he planned to murder her. Alice had showed up and pulled her from a clump of leaves that Nettleson had dumped over her. She dragged her to Pasquin's shed, with Nettleson chasing them a few yards behind.

A week later we sat in a conference room with Vernon, Loman, Tony, Marshall Long, Pasquin, and Gavi who had been rounded up rather reluctantly from Portu Landing. It was time to wrap things up, take statement from everyone, said Tony. Marshall had the most to say.

"The two World War II guns are pretty much identical except their land and groove markings. We can't be sure because we haven't found bullets in all cases, but we think the gun Nettleson stole was the one used on Jacob and Barley and Otis. The one used to shoot at you, Luanne, came from Alice's gun, the one not stolen. She shot at you, but didn't come near hitting you."

"Could have fooled me," I said.

"She wanted to scare you away from her man," said Tony. "She must have seen you around the little trailer."

Loman took up the story. "That old lady got about in a small motor boat she kept in that abandoned boat house. Her daddy taught her well." He nodded toward Gavi. "We found it just below Pasquin's place on the river. She must have seen or heard what was going on with Nettleson and the girl and pulled the boat in to help. Clever old bitty. We found syphoning tube in a bag in her boat. Probably stole the gas she needed to run up and down the river."

"Yet no one ever saw her," I said.

Pasquin chuckled. "Wouldn't. Clever enough to dodge prying eyes. Never broke the law by speeding, so who's going to stop her? Yeah, clever old swamp mistress."

"Her daddy taught her boats and guns and survival out here," said Gavi, his dark eyes lifting toward Tony. "She could have lived in those woods until her heart gave out."

"And where is she now?" I asked.

"The judge found her a room in a hospital about fifty miles from here," said Tony.

"The asylum, then?"

He nodded. The room remained silent for a long uncomfortable moment. Pasquin chuckled, a low throaty sound.

"That hospital is not too far from the Chattahoochee River. They better keep a close watch on her. She'll be out the door and disappeared before they know it."

CHAPTER TWENTY-THREE

Pasquin sat on my front porch, refusing to go inside and feel the central air.

"It rained today," he said, "cooled things down. You don't need all that artificial cold air blowing on you. You got river air." He spread his hands wide. Darkness would settle over the water in a few hours, and frogs would begin their songfest. Plato rested on the floor of the porch until Pasquin waved his hand in praise of nature. The dog leapt up and headed for the screen door. He needed no help opening it. Bounding down the steps he turned back once when I called his name. Giving an excited bark, he took off into the darkness.

"Might not be back until morning," said Pasquin.

"If then," I said. "Tomorrow is the fourth of July. I don't want him all freaked out when he hears firecrackers and roman candles go boom."

"That old dog scared of a few firecrackers? He stays out in some of the loudest thunder storms without going all sissy inside. Don't worry about him."

"I wonder how he does it, hangs out in all this weather."

"Same way old Alice did it. Know and love the place you're in. She turned herself loose, too. Stayed in a whole bunch of places, found her hospitality where she could. Even invented her own little rituals to deal with loss and celebration. Hell, how many old women do you know would throw off their clothes and run through the woods?"

"Plato must have been good company for her out there in the swamp."

"Most likely," said Pasquin. He took up his hat and fanned his ancient face. "Now that really was the man she should have been looking for, a swamp dog, the only kind she ever really needed."

We rocked in the silence when suddenly it was broken. Plato came running back down the rutted road, barking and wagging his tail. He leapt to the front steps and took up sentry duty there.

A truck was slowly bumping down the road. It pulled a flat bed trailer behind it. Atop the the trailer, locked in braces, sat a dark red canoe. When it came to a stop near the steps, a young man removed himself from the cab and pulled out a clip board.

"Miz Luanne Fogarty live here?"

I went down the steps. Plato ran about the truck and its trailer, sniffing and wagging and panting. Pasquin stood at the screen door, fanning himself with his hat.

"Sign here," said the young man.

"But…" I was confused. I hadn't rented another canoe.

"Sent by a Mr. Drake," he said and pointed to another signature on the paper. "Said it was a gift. Even had a name painted on the side."

"Vernon! God bless him," I said and signed the paper.

"Where do you want it, ma'am?"

I paused, then pointed to the river. "On the water. Where else?"

"Best lightweight we got. Seats two. Water ready. Oars are right there." He nodded to two oars that had been tied to a brace. I pulled them loose.

The man placed the canoe on the shore where I could shove it into the water. Its dark red paint was interrupted only at one point near one end with the words PEACE OFFERING. "Perfect name,"

I said.

"You don't think he meant to write 'peace officer' do you?" asked Pasquin who had moved to the landing.

"No. Peace offering is what he meant," I said and pushed the boat into the water. I climbed in and Plato jumped in behind me and began sniffing the bottom and sides. I rowed a few feet to deeper water.

"Rides like a dream," I said.

Plato aimed a bark to the approaching night. His front feet rested on one slat as he sniffed the air.

"Ready to ride, old boy?"

Recommended Memento Mori Mysteries

Luanne Fogarty mysteries by Glynn Marsh Alam
DIVE DEEP and DEADLY
DEEP WATER DEATH
COLD WATER CORPSE
RIVER WHISPERS (a literary novel)

Viv Powers mysteries by Letha Albright
DAREDEVIL'S APPRENTICE
BAD-LUCK WOMAN

A Katlin LaMar mystery by Sherri L. Board
BLIND BELIEF

Matty Madrid mysteries by P.J. Grady
MAXIMUM INSECURITY
DEADLY SIN

A Dr. Rebecca Temple mystery
by Sylvia Maultash Warsh
TO DIE IN SPRING

AN UNCERTAIN CURRENCY
Clyde Lynwood Sawyer, Jr.
Frances Witlin

A Suzanne LaFleshe Mystery by Hollis Seamon
FLESH

THE COLOR OF EMPTINESS
a crime novel by Cynthia Webb